'An easy **p** **occasiona** **part I work very long, very hard,'** **Owen stated.**

'Why? When you're wealthy enough to retire tomorrow?' Bella asked.

'Because I like it.' Because he couldn't not. Because he was driven. Because he was missing something that everyone else had—the compassion, the consideration, the plain awareness and empathy towards others. His relationship with Liz had made him feel claustrophobic. He wouldn't allow that pressure to be put on him again. But he'd have Bella the way he wanted.

'For all that *success*—' Owen underlined the word, knowing the concept annoyed her '—I'm still the guy who made your legs so weak you couldn't stand.' He took a step back, determined to walk away now. He spoke softer. 'I'm still the guy who made you alternately sigh then scream with pleasure.' He paused. He'd leave her knowing exactly what his intentions were—plain and simple. He spoke softer still. 'And I'm the guy who's going to do it all again.'

Dear Reader

Have you ever been in that awful awkward social situation where you felt totally out of place and just wished someone would come along and rescue you? Especially someone tall, dark and handsome, say? Wouldn't that make you look and feel like Miss Utterly Attractive herself?

Nice fantasy, isn't it? And Bella, my poor Bella, thought it might have actually happened to her!

But things are never quite as they are in fairytales, are they? Not everything goes as smoothly as we wish it would. And what if you do find your wish fulfilled? How do you handle it if it doesn't turn out to be all that you'd hoped?

Come and join Bella and Owen as they both discover that losing something they each thought precious might enable them to find something much, much better. Because there is nothing nicer than a happy ending and the beginning of a lifetime of love, is there?

I do hope you enjoy it!

Love

Natalie

PLEASURED IN THE PLAYBOY'S PENTHOUSE

BY
NATALIE ANDERSON

MILLS & BOON®

MODERN
Heat™

All the characters in this book have no existence outside the imagination
of the author, and have no relation whatsoever to anyone bearing the
same name or names. They are not even distantly inspired by any
individual known or unknown to the author, and all the incidents are
pure invention.

First published in Great Britain 2008
Harlequin Mills & Boon Limited,
Eton House, 18-24 Paradise Road, Richmond, Surrey TW9 1SR

© Natalie Anderson 2009

ISBN: 978 0 263 87235 4

Set in Times Roman 10½ on 12¾ pt
171-0209-50664

Printed and bound in Spain
by Litografia Rosés, S.A., Barcelona

Possibly the only librarian who got told off herself for talking too much, **Natalie Anderson** decided writing books might be more fun than shelving them—and boy, is it that. Especially writing romance—it's the realisation of a lifetime dream, kick-started by many an afternoon spent devouring Grandma's Mills & Boons®… She lives in New Zealand, with her husband and four gorgeous-but-exhausting children. Swing by her website any time—she'd love to hear from you: www.natalie-anderson.com

Recent titles by the same author:

BOUGHT: ONE NIGHT, ONE MARRIAGE
PLEASURED BY THE SECRET MILLIONAIRE
MISTRESS UNDER CONTRACT

For Soraya—you are so generous and supportive, always dropping everything to read in a rush and then getting back to me so quickly and so helpfully— and this one was some rush, wasn't it? I am really looking forward to repaying you in kind so very soon.

CHAPTER ONE

Dɪᴅ she want a 'sex machine' or a 'slow comfortable screw'? Choices, choices…and tonight Bella was struggling with decisions. The names were all such appalling puns, she didn't know if she'd be able to ask for one without blushing. Especially as she was sitting all alone in this bar—on a Friday night. The bartender would probably panic and think she was coming on to him. But as she looked at the gleaming glasses lined up behind the counter and the rows of bottles holding varying amounts of brightly coloured liquid, her taste buds were tickled. It had been a while since she'd had anything more indulgent than whatever was the cheapest red wine at the supermarket. Surely she was justified in having something fabulous to celebrate her day? And as this weekend had already burned one huge hole in her savings, she might as well make it a crater.

She looked back at the cocktail list, but barely read on. She'd waited all day for someone to say it. Someone. Anyone. It wasn't as if she expected a party—a cake, candles or even a card. It was a frantic time getting everything organised for Vita's wedding, Bella understood that. But surely even one of them could have remembered? Her father perhaps?

But no. She was just there, as usual, in the background, like the family cat. Present, accounted for, but blending in as if part of the furniture. It was only if she had some sort of catastrophe that they remembered her. And she was determined to avoid any catastrophes this weekend. This was Vita's special time. As uncomfortable as Bella felt, she was determined to help make the weekend as wonderful as it could be for her sister.

Volunteering to oversee the decorating had been her best idea. It had meant she'd been able to avoid most of the others. And honestly, she'd felt more at home with the waitresses and staff of the exclusive resort than with her own family and their friends.

When she'd paused at lunchtime she'd looked up and seen them out walking along the beach. The island of Waiheke looked as if it had been taken over by an accountancy convention. In truth it basically had. They were like clones. All wearing corporate casual. The men in fawn trousers and open-collared pale blue shirts. Tomorrow they'd be in fawn again only with white shirts for the wedding. Afterwards, they'd saunter on the sand in three-quarter 'casual' trousers, overly colourful Hawaiian shirts, with their pale feet sliding in leather 'mandals'. They all had crisp cut hair, and expensive sunglasses plastered across their faces. The women were using their even more expensive sunglasses to pin back their long, sleek hair. Her tall, glamorous cousins, her sister. They were all the same. All so incredibly successful—if you equated money, high-flying jobs and incredibly suitable partners with success.

She'd tried it once—to play it their way. She'd dated a guy who was more approved of by her own family than she was herself. What a disaster that had been. They still didn't believe that she'd been the one to end it. Of course, there were reasons for that. But none Bella felt like dwelling on now. Tomorrow was going to be bad enough.

After she'd finally hung all the ribbons on the white-shrouded chairs, she'd headed straight for the bar inside the main building of the hotel. She'd celebrate herself. Toast in another year. Raise a glass to the success of the last. Even if no one else was going to. Even if there wasn't that much success to toast.

There had been talk of a family dinner, but the preparations had run too late—drinks maybe. She was glad. She didn't want to face the all too inevitable questions about her career and her love-life, the looks of unwanted sympathy from her aunts. There'd be time enough for that the next day, when there was no way she could avoid them as much as she had today. For today was *her* day and she could spend the last of it however she wanted to.

Now, as she sat and waited to be served, she avoided looking around, pretending she was happy to be there alone. She pushed back the inadequacy with some mind games—she'd play a role and fake the confidence. She would do cosmopolitan woman—the woman who took on the world and played it her way. Who took no prisoners, had what she wanted and lived it to the max. It would be good practice for tomorrow when she'd be confronted by Rex and Celia. One of the fun things about being an actress—even a minor-league, bit-part player—was the pretending.

She read through the list again, muttering as she narrowed her choices. 'Do I want "sex on the beach" or a "screaming orgasm"?'

'Why do you have to choose?'

She turned her head sharply. There was a guy standing right beside her. One incredibly hot guy whom she knew she'd never seen before because she'd damn well remember if she had. Tall and dark and with the bluest of eyes capturing hers. While she was staring, he was talking some more.

'I would have thought a woman like you would always have both.'

Sex on the beach *and* a screaming orgasm? Looking up at him, she took a firmer grip on both the menu card and the sensation suddenly beating through her—the tantalising tempo of temptation.

He must be just about the only person here who wasn't involved in the wedding. Or maybe he was. He was probably one of her cousins' dates. For a split second disappointment washed through her. But then she looked him over again—he wasn't wearing an Armani suit and if he was one of their dates he'd definitely be in Armani. And he'd be hanging on his date's arm, not alone and possibly on the prowl in a bar. This guy was in jeans—the roughest fabric she'd seen in the place to date. They were wet around the ankles as if he'd been splashing in the water, and on his feet were a pair of ancient-looking boat shoes. A light grey long-sleeved tee shirt covered his top half. It had a slight vee at the neck, exposing the base of the tanned column that was his neck. It was such a relief to see someone doing truly casual—someone not flaunting evidence of their superb bank balance.

Those bright blue eyes smiled at her. Very brightly. And then they looked her up and down.

Suddenly she felt totally uncomfortable as she thought about her own appearance. Not for the first time she wished for the cool, glamorous gene that the rest of her family had inherited. Instead she was hot, mosquito bitten, with a stripe of cooked-lobster-red sunburn across one half of her chest where she'd missed with her 110 SPF sunscreen. Her white cotton blouse was more off-white than bright and the fire-engine-red ribbon of her floral skirt was starting to come loose—but that was what you got for wearing second-hand.

It was one of her more sedate outfits, an attempt to dress up a little, in deference to the 'family' and their expectations. She'd even used the hotel iron—a real concession given she usually got at least one burn when she went anywhere near the things. Today had been no different. There was a small, very red, very sore patch just below her elbow. And now, thanks to a day spent on her knees dressing chairs in white robes and yellow ribbons, she knew she looked a sight.

As she took in his beautifully chiselled jaw, she really wished she'd bothered to go to her room and check her face or something on the way. There'd been some mascara on her eyelashes this morning, a rub of lip balm. Both were undoubtedly long gone. She was hardly in a state to be drawing single guys to her across a bar. She darted a glance around. She was the only female in the room. And there were only a couple of other customers. Then she looked at her watch. It was early. He was just making small talk with the only woman about. He was probably a travelling salesman. Only he definitely didn't look the salesman type. And despite the suggestion in his talk he didn't come across as sleazy. There was a bit of a glint in those blue eyes—she'd like to think it was appreciation, but it was more of a dare. And there was more humour than anything. She could do with some humour.

The bartender came back down to where they were standing. And Bella took up the challenge. Cosmopolitan woman she would be. Summoning all her courage and telling her cheeks to remain free of excess colour, she ordered. 'A "sex on the beach" and a "screaming orgasm" please.'

She refused to look at him but she could sense his smile of approval—could hear it in his voice as he ordered too.

'I'll have two "screaming orgasms" and "sex on the beach".'

Bella studiously watched the bartender line up the five shot glasses. She didn't want to turn and look in his eyes again, not entirely sure she wouldn't be mesmerised completely. But peripheral vision was very handy. She was motionless, seemingly fixated on the bartender as he carefully poured in each ingredient, but in reality she was wholly focused on the guy next to her as he pulled out the bar stool next to hers and sat on it. His leg brushed against hers as he did. It was a very long leg, and it looked fine clad in the faded denim. She could feel the strength just from that one accidental touch.

Silently, shaking inside, she went to lift the first glass in the line-up. But then his hand covered hers, lightly pressing it down to the wood. Did he feel her fingers jerk beneath his? She snatched a moment to recover her self-possession before attempting to look at him with what she hoped was sophisticated query.

His bright blues were twinkling. 'Have the orgasm first.'

She could feel the heat as her blood beat its way to her cheeks.

The twinkles in his eyes burned brighter. 'After all, you can always have another one later.'

She stared at him as he released her. He'd turned on the widest, laziest, most sensual smile she'd ever seen. Spellbound wasn't the word. Almost without thinking, she moved her fingers, encircling the second shot.

'What about you?' Why had her voice suddenly gone whispery?

'A gentleman always lets the lady go first.'

So she picked up the orgasm, kind of amazed her hand wasn't visibly trembling. In a swift motion she knocked the contents back into her mouth and swallowed the lot. She took a moment before breathing—then it was a short, sharp breath as she absorbed the burning hit. Slowly she put the glass back down on the bar.

His smile was wicked now. He'd picked up the sex shot, pausing pointedly with it slightly raised, until she did the same. She met his eyes and lifted the glass to her lips. Simultaneously they tipped back and swallowed.

Slamming his on the bench, he picked up the next shot. Then he paused again, inclined his head towards the remaining orgasm.

'You know it's for you.' That smile twisted his mouth as he spoke and its teasing warmth reached out to her.

There was no way she could refuse. She couldn't actually speak for the fire in her throat. So she picked up the shot and again, eyes trained on him, drank. And he mirrored her, barely half a beat behind.

It was a long, deep breath she drew that time. And her recovery was much slower. She stared for a while at the five empty glasses in front of them. And then she looked back at him.

He wasn't smiling any more. At least, his mouth wasn't turned up. But his eyes searched hers while sending a message at the same time. And the warmth was all pervasive. The burning sensation rippled through her body, showing no sign of cooling. Instead her temperature was still rising. And she wasn't at all sure if it was from the alcohol or the fire in his gaze.

Wow. She tried to take another deep breath. But the cool of the air made her tingling lips sizzle more. His gaze dropped to her mouth as if he knew of her sensitivity. The sizzle didn't cease.

She blinked, pressed her lips together to try to stop the whisper of temptation they were screaming to her, resumed visual contemplation of the empty shot glasses. She should never have looked at him.

'Thank you,' she managed, studying him peripherally again.

He shrugged, mouth twitching, lightening the atmosphere and making her wonder if she'd overemphasised that supercharged moment. Of course there was no way he would be hitting on her. Now his eyes said it was all just a joke. As if he knew that if she thought he was really after her, she'd be running a mile. City slicker vixen-in-a-bar was so not her style. But she'd decided anything could be possible tonight. Anything she wanted could be hers. She was pretending, remember?

'So are we celebrating, or drowning sorrows?' He flashed that easy smile again. And it gave her the confidence that up until now she'd been faking.

'Celebrating.' She turned to face him.

His brows raised. She could understand his surprise. People didn't usually celebrate in a bar drinking *all by themselves*. So she elaborated.

'It's my birthday.'

'Oh? Which one?'

Did the man not know it was rude to ask? She nearly giggled. But he was so gorgeous she decided to forgive him immediately. Besides, she had the feeling his boldness was innate. It was simply him. It gave her another charge. 'My flirtieth.'

'I'm sorry?' She could see the corners of his mouth twitching again.

'My flirtieth.' So she was making an idiot of herself. What did she care? This night was hers and she could do as she wanted with it—and that might just include flirting with strangers.

'You're either lying or lisping. I think maybe both.' His lips quirked again. And the thing was, she didn't find it offensive.

So he was laughing at her. It was worth it just to see the way that smile reached right into his eyes.

'How many have you had?' he asked. 'You seem to be slurring.'

Not only that, she was still staring fixedly at him. She forced herself to blink again. It was so hard not to look at him. His was a face that captured attention and held it for ever. 'These were my first.'

'And last.' He called the bartender over and ordered. 'Sedate white wine spritzer, please.'

'Who wants sedate?' she argued, ignoring his further instructions to the waiter. 'The last thing I want is wine.' The urge for something stronger gripped her—something even more powerful, something to really take her breath away. She wanted the taste of fire to take away the lonely bitterness of disappointment.

'Not true. Come on, whine away. Why are you here, celebrating alone?'

He'd do. The blue in his eyes was all fire.

'I'm not alone. My family is here too—my sister is getting married tomorrow in the resort.'

His brows flashed upwards again. 'So why aren't they here now celebrating your birthday with you?'

She paused. A chink in her act was about to be revealed, but she answered honestly. 'They've forgotten.'

'Ah.' He looked at her, only a half-smile now. 'So the birthday girl has missed out on her party.'

She shrugged. 'Everyone's been busy with the wedding.'

The spritzer arrived, together with a bottle of wine for him and two tall glasses of water.

'Tell me about this wedding.' He said wedding as if it were a bad word.

'What's to tell? She's gorgeous. He's gorgeous. A suc-cessful, wealthy, nice guy.'

He inclined his head towards her. 'And you're a little jealous?'

'No!' She shook her head, but a little hurt stabbed inside. She wasn't jealous of Vita, surely she wasn't. She was truly pleased for her. And no way on this earth would she want Hamish. 'He's solid and dependable.' The truth came out. 'Square.'

'You don't like square?'

She thought about it. Hamish *was* a nice person. And he thought the world of Vita—you could see it in the way he looked at her. He adored her. That little hurt stabbed again. She toughed it out. 'I like a guy who can make me laugh.'

'Do you, now?' But he was the one who laughed. A low chuckle that made her want to smile too—if she weren't having a self-piteous moment. He sobered. 'What's your role in the wedding?'

'Chief bridesmaid,' she said mournfully.

His warm laughter rumbled again.

'It's all right for you,' she said indignantly. 'You've never been a bridesmaid.'

'And you have?'

She nodded. It was all too hideous. 'I know all about it. This is my fourth outing.'

And, yes, she knew what they said. Three times a brides-maid and all that. Her aunts would be reminding her tomorrow. The only one of her siblings not perfectly paired off.

'What's the best man like?'

She couldn't hide the wince. Rex. How unfortunate that Hamish's best friend was the guy Bella had once picked in her weak moment of trying to be all that the family wanted.

'That bad, huh?'

'Worse.' Because after she'd broken up with him—and it had been her—he'd started dating her most perfect cousin of them all, Celia. And no one in the family could believe that Bella would dump such a catch as Rex and so it was that she earned even more sympathy—more shakes of the head. Not only could she not hold down a decent job, she couldn't hold onto a decent man. No wonder her father treated her like a child. She supposed, despite her Masters degree and her array of part-time jobs, she was. She still hadn't left home, was still dependent on the old man for the basics—like food.

'So.' Her charming companion at the bar speared her attention again with a laser-like look. 'Invite me.'

'I'm sorry?'

'You're the chief bridesmaid, aren't you? You've got to have a date for the wedding.'

'I'm not going to invite a total stranger to my sister's wedding.'

'Why not? It'll make it interesting.'

'How so?' she asked. 'Because you're really a psycho out to create mayhem?'

He laughed at that. 'Look, it's pretty clear you're not looking forward to it. They've forgotten your birthday. This isn't about them. This is about you doing something you want to. Do something you think is tempting.'

'You think you're tempting?' OK, so he was. He sure was. But *he* didn't need to be so sure about it.

He leaned forward. 'I think what tempts you is the thought of doing something unexpected.'

He was daring her. She very nearly smiled then. It would be too—totally unexpected. And the idea really appealed to her. It had been her motivation all evening—for most of her life, in fact. To be utterly unlike the staid, conservative perfectionists in her bean-counter family. And how wonderful it would be to turn up on the arm of the most handsome man she'd ever seen. Pure fantasy. Especially when she was the only one of the younger generation not to be in a happy couple and have a high-powered career.

And then, for once, she had a flash of her father's conservatism—of realism. 'I can't ask you. I barely know you.'

He leaned forward another inch. 'But you have all night to get to know me.'

CHAPTER TWO

ALL night? Now it was Bella's lips twitching.

His smile was wicked. 'Come on. Ask me anything.'

Holding his gaze was something she wasn't capable of any more. She ducked it, sat back and concentrated on the conversation.

'All right. Are you married?' She'd better establish the basics.

'Never have, never will.'

Uh-huh. 'Live-in lover?'

'Heaven forbid.'

She paused. He was letting her know exactly where he stood on the commitment front. Devilry danced in his eyes. She knew he meant every word, but she also knew he was challenging her to pull him up on it.

'Gay?' she asked blithely.

He looked smugly amused. 'Will you take my word for it or do you want proof?'

Now *there* was a challenge. And not one she was up for just yet.

'Diseases?' Tart this time.

His amusement deepened. 'I think there's diabetes on my father's side, but that doesn't seem to manifest until old age.'

She refused to smile, was determined to find some flaw. To get the better of him somehow. 'What do you do for a living?'

'I work with computers.'

Gee, she nearly snorted, that could mean anything. 'Computers? As in programming?'

His head angled and for the first time his gaze slid from hers. 'Sort of.'

'Ah-h-h.' She nodded, as if it all made perfect sense. Then she wrinkled her nose.

'Ah, what?' He sat up straighter. 'Why the disapproval?'

She hit him then, with everything she could think of. 'Did you know the people most likely to download porn are single, male computer nerds aged between twenty-five and thirty-five? You've probably got some warped perception of the female body now, right? And I bet you're into games—with those female characters with boobs bigger than bazookas and skinny hips and who can knock out five hit men in three seconds.' She stopped for breath, dared him to meet *her* challenge.

'Ah.' His smile widened while his eyes promised retribution. 'Well, actually, no, that's not me.'

'You think?' she asked innocently.

'I'm single, I'm male, I'm into computers and I'm aged between twenty-five and thirty-five. But I don't need porn because…' he leaned closer and whispered '…I'm not a nerd.'

She leaned a little closer, whispered right back. 'That's what you think.' Admittedly he didn't look much like one, but she could bluff.

But then he called her on it. Laughing aloud, he asked, 'Should I be wearing glasses and have long, lank, greasy hair?'

His hair was short and wind-spiked and his eyes were bright, perceptive and unadorned—and suddenly they flashed with glee.

'Do nerds have muscles like these?' He slapped his bicep with his hand. 'Go on, feel them.'

She could hardly refuse when she'd been the one to throw the insult. Tentatively she reached out a hand and poked gingerly at his upper arm with her finger. It was rock hard. Intrigued, she took a second shot. Spread her fingers wide, pressing down on the grey sleeve. Underneath was big, solid muscle. Really big. And she could feel the definition, was totally tempted to feel further...

But she pulled back, because there was a sudden fire streaming through her. She must be blushing something awful. She took a much-needed sip of her watered-down wine.

His told-you-so gaze teased her.

She sniffed. 'You're probably wearing a body suit under that shirt.' Completely clutching at straws.

'OK,' he said calmly, 'feel them now.' He took her hand, lifted the hem of his shirt and before she knew it her palm was pressed to his bare abs.

OK? Hell, yes, OK!

She froze. Her mind froze. Her whole body froze. But her hand didn't. The skin on his stomach was warm and beneath her fingers she could feel the light scratchiness of hair and then the rock-hard indents of muscles. This was no weedy-boy-who-spent-hours-in-front-of-a-computer physique. And this wasn't just big, strong male. This was fit. *Superfit.*

Her fingers badly wanted to stretch out some more and explore. If she moved her thumb a fraction she'd be able to stroke below his navel. She whipped her hand out while she still had it under control.

His smile was wicked as the heat in her cheeks became unbearable. 'And what about this tan, hmm?' He pushed up a sleeve and displayed a bronzed forearm as if it were some treasured museum exhibit. She stared at the length of it, lightly hair-dusted, muscle flexing, she could see the clear outline of a thick vein running down to the back of a very broad palm. Very real, very much alive—and strong. She was taken with his hand for some time.

Finally she got back the ability to speak. 'Is the tan all-over-body?'

'If you're lucky you might get to find out.'

The guy had some nerve. But he was laughing as he said it.

'So why are you single, then?' she said, trying to adopt an acidic tone. 'I mean, if you're such a catch, why haven't you been caught already?'

'You misunderstand the game, sweetheart,' he answered softly. 'I'm not the prey. I'm the predator.'

And if she could bring herself to admit it, she wanted him to pounce on her right now. But she was still working on defence and denial. 'Well, you're not that good, then, are you? Where's your catch tonight?'

The only answer was a quick lift of his brows and a wink.

She pressed her lips together, but couldn't quite stop them quirking upwards. 'You hunt often?'

He laughed outright at that, shaking his head. She wasn't sure if it was a negative to her question or simple disbelief at the conversation in general. 'I'm like a big-game animal—one hunt will last me some time.' His eyes caught hers again. 'And I only hunt when I see something really, really juicy.'

Juicy, huh? Her juices were running now and that voice in her head saying 'eat me' really should be shot.

His laughter resurfaced, though not as loud, and she knew he'd twigged her thoughts.

Still she refused to join in. 'But you don't keep your catches.'

'No.' He shook his head. 'Catch and release. That's the rule.'

Hmm. Bella wasn't so sure about the strategy. 'What if she doesn't want to be released?'

'Ah, but she does,' he corrected. 'Because she understands the rules of the game. And even if she doesn't, it won't take long until she wants out.'

Her mouth dropped. She couldn't imagine any woman wanting to get away from this guy's net. Flirting outrageously was too much fun—especially when the flirt had a body like this and eyes like those.

His smile sharpened round the edges. 'I have it on good authority that I'm *very* selfish.'

'Ah-h-h.' She was intrigued. That smacked of bitter-ex-girlfriend speak. Was he playing the field on the rebound? 'You've never wanted to catch and keep?'

He grimaced. 'No.'

'Why not?'

For the first time he looked serious. 'Nothing *keeps*. Things don't ever stay the same.' He paused, the glint resurfaced. 'The answer is to go for what you want, when you want it.'

'And after that?'

He didn't reply, merely shrugged his shoulders.

Bella took another sip of the spritzer and contemplated what she knew to be the ultimate temptation before her—defence and denial crumbling. 'After that' didn't matter really, did it? He had a beautiful body and a sense of humour—what more would a confident, cosmopolitan woman want for an evening? And wasn't that what she was—for tonight?

'So, now that you know something about me,' he said, 'tell me, what do *you* do?'

He might have told her some things, but strangely she felt as if she knew even less. But what she really wanted to know, he didn't need words for. She wanted to know if that tan was all-over-body, she wanted to know the heat and strength of those muscles—the feel of them. Everything of him. Cosmo woman here she was.

'I'm an actor,' she declared, chin high.

There was a pause. 'Ah-h-h.'

'Ah, what?' She didn't like the look of his exaggerated, knowing nod.

'I bet you're a very good one,' he sidestepped.

Her cosmo confidence ebbed. 'I could be.' Given the opportunity.

'Could?'

'Sure.' She just needed that lucky break.

Now he was looking way too amused. 'What else do you do?'

'What do you mean what else?' she snapped. 'I'm an actor.'

'I don't know of many actors who don't have some sort of day job.'

She sighed—totally theatrically, and then capitulated. 'I make really good coffee.'

He laughed again. 'Of course you do.'

Of course. She was the walking cliché. The family joke. The wannabe. And no way in hell was she telling him what else she did. Children's birthday party entertainer ranked as one of the lowest, most laughable occupations on the earth— her family gave her no end of grief about it. She didn't need to give him more reason to as well.

'And how is the life of a jobbing actor these days?' He was still looking a tad too cynically amused for her liking.

She sighed again—doubly theatrical. 'I have "the nose".'

'"The nose"?'

She turned her head, offered him a profile shot.

He studied it seriously for several seconds. Then, 'What's wrong with it?'

'A little long, a little straight.'

'I'd say it's majestic.'

She jumped when he ran his finger down it. The tip tingled as he tapped it.

'Quite,' she acknowledged, sitting back out of reach. 'It gives me character and that's what I am—a character actress.'

'I'm not convinced it's the nose that makes you so full of character,' he drawled.

'Quite.' She almost laughed—it was taking everything to ignore his irony. 'I've not the looks for the heroine. I'm the sidekick.'

She didn't mention it, but there was also the fact she was on the rounder side of skinny. A little short, a little curvy for anything like Hollywood. But Wellywood—more formally known as Wellington, New Zealand's own movie town? Maybe. She just needed to get the guts to move there.

'Oh, I wouldn't say—'

'Don't.' She raised her hand, stopped him mid-sentence. 'It's true. No leading-lady looks here, but it doesn't matter because the smart-ass sidekick gets all the best lines anyway.'

'But not the guy.'

She frowned. So true. And half the time she didn't get the sidekick part either. She got the walk-on-here, quick-exit-there parts. The no-name ones that never earned any money, fame or even notoriety.

She figured it was because she hadn't done the posh drama academy thing. Her father had put his foot down. She wasn't to waste her brain on that piffle—a hobby sure, but never a career. So she'd been packed off to university—like all her siblings. Only instead of brain-addling accountancy or law, she'd read English. And, to her father's horror, film studies. After a while he'd 'supposed she might go into teaching'.

He'd supposed wrong. She'd done evening classes in acting at the local high school. Read every method book in the library. Watched the classic films a million kazillion times. Only at all those agencies and casting calls it was almost always the same talent turning up and she couldn't help but be psyched out by the pros, by the natural talents who'd been onstage from the age of three and who had all the confidence and self-belief in the world.

Bella thought she had self-belief. But it fought a hard battle against the disbelief of her family. 'When are you going to settle into a real job?' they constantly asked. 'This drama thing is just a hobby. You don't want to be standing on your feet making coffee, or blowing up balloons for spoilt toddlers for the rest of your days…' And on and on and on.

'Well, who wants the guy anyway?' she asked grumpily. 'I don't want the saccharine love story. Give me adventure and snappy repartee any day.'

'Really?' he asked in total disbelief. 'You sure you don't want the big, fluffy princess part?'

'No, Prince Charming is boring.' And Prince Charming, the guy her family had adored, wouldn't let her be herself.

He leaned forward, took her chin in his hand and turned her to face him. 'I don't believe you're always this cynical.'

The comment struck another little stab into her. It twisted a little sharper when she saw he was totally serious.

'No,' she admitted honestly. 'Only when it's my birthday and no one has remembered and I'm stuck in wedding-of-the-century hell.'

'All weddings are hell.' His fingers left her face but his focus didn't.

Well, this one sure was. 'Here was me thinking it was going to be a barefoot-on-the-beach number with hardly anyone in attendance, but it's massive—ninety-nine per cent of the resort is booked out with all the guests!'

'Hmm.' He was silent a moment. Then he flicked her a sideways glance. 'How lucky for you that I'm in that remaining one per cent.'

Wordless, she stared at him, taking a second to believe the lazy arrogance in the comment he'd so dryly delivered. Then she saw the teasing, over-the-top wink.

Her face broke and the amusement burst forth.

'Finally!' He spoke above her giggles. 'She laughs. And when she laughs…'

The laughter passed between them, light and fresh, low and sweet. And her mood totally lifted.

'I am so sorry,' she apologised, shaking her head.

'That's OK. You're clearly having a trying day.'

'Something like that.' The thought of tomorrow hadn't made it any easier and she'd felt guilty for feeling so me-me-me that it had all compounded into a serious case of the grumps.

'Shall we start over?' His eyes were twinkling again and this time she didn't try to stop her answering smile.

'Please, that would be good.' And it would be good. Because it was quite clear that under his super-flirt exterior there was actually a nice guy. Not to mention, damn attractive.

'I'm Owen Hughes. Disease-free, single and straight.'

Owen. A player to be sure—but one that she knew would be a lot of fun.

'I'm Bella Cotton. Also disease-free, single and straight.'

'Bella,' he repeated, but didn't make the obvious 'beautiful' translation. He didn't need to—simply the way he said it made her feel its meaning. Then he made her smile some more. 'Any chance you're in need of a laugh?'

She nodded. 'Desperately. Light relief is what I need.'

'I can do that.' He grinned again and she found herself feeling happier than she had all day—all week even. He leaned towards her. 'Look, I've got an empty pit instead of a stomach right now. Have dinner with me—unless you've got some full-on rehearsal dinner to go to or something?'

She shook her head. 'Amazingly that's not the plan. I think some of the younger guests are just supposed to meet up later for drinks. The olds are doing their own thing.'

'Maybe they've organised a surprise birthday party for you.'

'As nice as that idea sounds—' and it did sound really nice '—they haven't. You can trust me on that.'

'OK. Then let's go find a table.'

She found herself standing and walking with him to the adjoining restaurant just like that. No hesitation, no second thought, just simplicity.

He grinned as they sat down. 'I really am starving.'

'So you haven't caught anything much lately, you big tiger, you,' she mocked.

He laughed. 'I'm confident I can make up for it.'

Bella met the message in his eyes. And was quite sure he could.

CHAPTER THREE

OWEN felt a ridiculous surge of pleasure at finally having made Bella see the funny side. And, just as he'd suspected, she had a killer of a smile and a deadly sweet giggle. Her full lips invited and her eyes crinkled at the corners. He couldn't decide if they were pale blue or grey, but he liked looking a lot while trying to work it out and he liked watching them widen the more he looked.

He'd been bluffing—if he really were some tiger in the jungle, he'd have died of starvation months ago. Sex was a recreational hobby for him, very recreational. But it had been a while. Way too much of a while. Maybe that was why he'd felt the irresistible pull of attraction when she'd walked into the bar. He'd been sitting at a table in the corner and almost without will had walked up to stand beside her at the bar. Just to get a closer look at her little hourglass figure. In the shirt and skirt he could see shapely legs and frankly bountiful breasts that had called to the most base of elements in him.

Then he'd noticed the droop to her lip that she'd been determinedly trying to lift as she'd read that menu. And he'd just had to make her smile.

The table he'd led her to was in the most isolated corner of the restaurant he could find. He didn't want her family interrupting any sooner than necessary. Wanted to keep jousting and joking with her. Wanted a whole lot more than that too and needed the time to make it happen.

'So,' she asked, suddenly perky, 'what sort of computers? You work for some software giant?'

'I work for myself.' For the last ten years he'd done nothing much other than work—pulling it together, thinking it through, organising the team and getting it done.

'Programming what—games? Banking software?'

'I work in security.'

'Oh, my.' She rolled her eyes. 'I bet you're one of them whiz-kids who broke into the FBI's files when you were fourteen, or created some nasty virus. Bad-boy hacker now crossed over to the good side or something—am I right?'

'No.' He chuckled. Truth was the actual programming stuff wasn't him—he had bona fide computer nerds working for him. He was the ideas guy—who'd thought up a way to make online payments more secure, and now to protect identity. 'I've never been in trouble with the law.'

'Oh. So…' She paused, clearly trying to think up the next big assault. 'Business good?'

'You could say that.' Inwardly he smiled. He now had employees scattered around the world. A truly international operation, but one that he preferred to direct from his inner-city bolt hole in Wellington. But he didn't want to talk about work—it was all consuming, even keeping his mind racing when he should be asleep. That was why he was on Waiheke, staying at his holiday home a few yards down the beach from the hotel. He was due for some R & R, a little distraction. And the ideal distraction seemed to have stepped right in front of him.

His banter before hadn't all been a lie, though. He did

believe in going for what he wanted and then moving right on. This little poppet was the perfect pastime for his weekend of unwind time. So he'd made sure she understood the way he played it. Spelt the rules out loud and clear. She'd got them, as he'd intended, and she was tempted. Now he just had to give her that extra little nudge.

She was studying the menu intently. And he studied her, taken by the stripe of sunburn that disappeared under her shirt. It seemed to be riding along to the crest of her breast and his fingers itched to follow its path.

When the waiter came she ordered with an almost reckless abandonment and he joined in. He *was* hungry. He'd splashed up the beach over an hour ago now. He hadn't been able to be bothered fixing something for himself, figured he'd get a meal to take away from the restaurant. Only now he'd found something better to take back with him.

'Oh, no.' The look on her face was comical.

'What?' he asked.

'Some of my family has arrived.'

'It's time for drinks, then, huh?' He turned his head in the direction she was staring. Inwardly cursing. Just when she was getting warmed up.

He saw the tall blonde looking over at them speculatively. When she saw them notice her, she strode over, long legs making short work of the distance.

'Bella. So sorry,' she clipped. 'It's your birthday and you're here all alone.'

What? thought Owen. Was he suddenly invisible?

'I can't believe you didn't remind us,' the blonde continued, still ignoring him.

'I didn't want to say anything.' For a second he saw the pain in Bella's eyes. A surge of anger hit him.

He realised what she'd done. She'd tested them. And they'd failed.

'Don't worry.' He spoke up. 'She's not alone. It's just that we wanted to have our own private celebration.'

The blonde looked at him then, frosty faced. 'And you are?'

'Owen,' he answered, as if that explained it all.

'Owen.' She glanced to Bella and then back to give him the once-over. He watched her coldness thaw to a sugary smile as she checked out his watch and his shoes. He knew she recognised the brands. Yes, darling, he thought, I'm loaded. And it was one thing Bella *hadn't* noticed. He found it refreshing.

'It seems you've been keeping a few things to yourself lately, Isabella.'

Owen looked at Bella. There was a plea in her eyes he couldn't ignore.

The silence deepened, becoming more awkward as he kept his focus on her. And a tinge of amusement tugged when finally the willowy blonde spoke, sounding disconcerted. 'I'll leave you to your meal, then.'

'Thank you,' Owen answered, not taking his gaze off Bella. He was never normally so rude, but he could do arrogance when necessary. And when he'd seen the hurt in Bella's eyes he'd known it was necessary. The irrational need to help her, to support her, had bitten him. Stupid. Because Owen wasn't the sort to do support. Ordinarily he did all he could to avoid any show of interest or involvement other than the purely physical, purely fun. He'd made that mistake before and been pushed too close to commitment as a result. His ex-girlfriend had wanted the ring, the ceremony, the works. He hadn't. But then she'd tried to force it in a way he totally resented her for. The experience had been so bad he was determined to make damn sure it didn't happen again. He no longer had relationships. He had flings.

But now he simply hoped that his brush-off would be reported back to the rest of the family and they'd all stay away for a bit.

The waiter arrived with the first plates, breaking the moment. Bella was busy picking up her fork, but he could see her struggling to hold back her smile.

He waited until she'd swallowed her first bite. 'Am I invited now?'

'If I do, your job is to entertain me, right?' Her smile was freed. 'No eyeing up my beautiful cousins.'

He didn't need anyone else to eye up. And he'd entertain her all night and then some if she wanted. But he played the tease some more. 'How beautiful are they?'

She stared down her majestic nose at him. 'You just met one of them.'

'Her?' he asked, putting on surprise. 'She's not beautiful.'

Her expression of disbelief was magic.

He laughed. 'She's not. So she's tall and blonde. So what? They're a dime a dozen. I'd far rather spend time with someone interesting.' He'd done tall and blonde many times over in his past. These days he was searching for something a little different.

She ignored him. 'No getting wildly drunk and embarrassing me. That isn't why you want to go, is it? The free booze?'

'No.'

'Then why?'

The truth slipped out. 'I want to see you have a really good time. A really, really good time.'

He did too. And he knew he could give it to her, and how. There was a baseline sizzle between them that was intense and undeniable. He'd seen the recognition, the jolt of awareness in her expression the moment their gazes had first locked. It was what she needed; it was what he needed. And he'd happily spend the weekend at her dull family wedding to get it. He'd put up with a lot more to get it if he had to.

On top of that primary, physical attraction, she was funny. Smart. Definitely a little bitter. And he liked her smile. He liked to make her smile.

As their dinner progressed it was nice to forget about everything for a moment as he concentrated wholly on her. He pulled his mobile out of his pocket and flicked it to Vibrate, pushing work from his mind. He was supposed to be having a couple of hours off after all. Like forty-eight.

He saw her glance into the main body of the restaurant as it filled. Saw her attention turn from him to whatever the deal was about tomorrow.

'It's going to be a massive wedding,' she said gloomily. 'The whole family and extended family and friends and everyone.'

'All that fuss for nothing.' He just couldn't see the point of it. Nor could he see why it was such a problem for her.

'All that money for just one day.' She shook her head. Her hair feathered out; shoulder length, it was a light wavy brown. He wanted to lean over and feel it fly over his face.

'Do you know how much she's spent on the dress?'

So money was some of it. 'I hate to think.' His drollery seemed to pass her by.

'And I've got the most hideous bridesmaid's dress. Hideous.'

'You'll look gorgeous.' She was such a cute package she could wear anything and look good.

'You don't understand,' she said mournfully. 'It's a cast of thousands. Celia—the gorgeous cousin—is one too. And there are others.' The little frown was back.

Her every emotion seemed to play out on her face—she was highly readable. If she could control it, learn to manipulate it, then she'd make a very good actress.

'The dress suits all of them, of course.'

'Of course.' And she was worried about what she looked like—what woman wasn't? He'd be happy to reassure her, spend some time emphasising her most favourable assets.

She looked up at him balefully. 'They're all five-seven or more and svelte.'

Whereas she was maybe five-four and all curves. He'd have her over ten tall blonde Celias any day.

'Did they go with a gift list?' He played along.

'Yes.' She ground out the answer. 'The cheapest item was just under a hundred bucks—and you had to buy a pair.'

Money was definitely an issue. He supposed it must be— fledgling actresses and café staff didn't exactly earn lots. And this resort was one of the most exclusive and expensive in the country. To be having a wedding here meant someone had some serious dosh. Was she worried about not keeping up with the family success?

He laughed, wanting to keep the mood light. 'Lists are such a waste of time. They'd be better off leaving it to chance and getting two coffee plungers. That way when they split up they can have one each.'

Surprise flashed on her face. 'Oh, and you call *me* cynical.'

'Marriage isn't worth the paper it's written on.' He'd been witness to that one all right—hit on the head with a sledge-hammer. It was all a sham.

'You think?'

'Come on, how many people make it to ten years these days, seven even? What's the point?' Because at some point, *always*, it ended. Owen figured it was better to walk before the boredom or the bitterness set in—and it would set in. The feelings never lasted—he'd seen that, he'd felt it himself. Now he knew it was better not to get tied into something you didn't want—and certainly not to drag the lives of innocents into it either. He wasn't running the risk of that happening ever again. No live-in lover, no wife, no kids.

Bella sat back and thought. She had to give him that—one of her older cousins had separated only last month, a marriage of three and a half years over already. But other marriages worked out, didn't they? She had high hopes for Vita and Hamish. She had faint hopes for herself—if she was lucky.

She frowned at him. 'Yes, we already know it's not on your agenda.' He couldn't commit to marriage—the monogamy bit would get him. He was too buff to be limited to one woman. Smorgasbord was his style. Well, that was fine. She was hardly at a 'settle down' point in life. She was still working on the *'get'* a life bit.

'That's right.' He grinned. 'But I'm not averse to helping others celebrate their folly.'

'So you can flirt with all the bridesmaids?' A little dig.

'Not all of them. Just one.'

The shorter, darker-haired, dumpier one with the long straight nose? He was just being nice because he hadn't actually *seen* all the others yet. When he did, it would be all over. She looked up from her cleared plate and encountered his stare again. The glint was back and notch by notch making her smoulder.

His stare didn't waver. And the message grew stronger.

Pure want.

She curled her fingers around her chilled wine glass. She felt flushed all over and had the almost desperate thought that she needed to cool down. Her fingers tightened. Then his hand covered hers, holding the glass to the table.

'I think you've had enough.'

She narrowed her eyes, unsure of his meaning.

He lifted his hands, spread his fingers as he shrugged loosely. 'I'm not suggesting you're drunk. Far from it.' His smile flashed, and it was all wicked. 'But the more you drink, the duller your senses become and I wouldn't want you to lose any sensation. Not tonight.'

'I'm going to need my senses?' She was mesmerised.

'All of them.'

OK.

He inclined his head to the large bi-folding doors that opened out to the deck. A small jazz ensemble was playing. She hadn't even noticed them set up. Too focused on her companion—the most casual customer in the place yet the one who commanded all her attention.

'Dance with me.' He stood. 'We can see how well we move together. Make sure we've got it right for the big day tomorrow.'

Why did she take everything he said and think he was really meaning something else?

He grinned, seeming to understand her problem exactly, and silently telling her that she was absolutely right. He held out his hand.

For a split second she looked at it. The broad palm, the long fingers, the invitation. The instant she placed her hand on top, he locked it into his. There was no going back now.

They walked out the doors together, to the part of the deck by the band where people were dancing. The waves were gently washing the beach. The evening was warm and for Bella the night seemed to exude magic.

'I like this old music,' he muttered, curling one arm around her waist while holding her hand to his chest with the other. 'Made for my kind of dancing.'

'Your kind?'

'Where you actually touch.' His hand was wide and firm across the small of her back as he pulled her towards him, and she went to him because she couldn't not. Because in reality she wanted to get closer still. Her head barely reached above his shoulders, but it didn't matter because she couldn't focus much further than on the material right in front of her anyway, and on the inviting, warm strength beneath it.

His fingers feathered over her back, skin to skin. She trembled at the sensation, nearly stumbled with the need that rose deep within her. She masked the craziness of her response with some sarcasm. 'I said yes to dancing, not having your hands up my shirt.'

'I thought up your shirt might be quite good.' His low reply in her ear made her need heighten to almost painful intensity.

Good was an understatement. He pressed her that little bit closer, so her breasts were only a millimetre from the hard wall that was his chest. Not quite close enough to touch, but she could almost, almost feel him and her nipples were tight.

She dragged in a burning breath. 'Owen, I—'

'Shh,' he said. 'Your family is watching.'

He danced her away from the others and into the farthest corner of the deck, where the darkness of night lurked, encroaching on the lights and loud conviviality of the restaurant. Gently he swayed them both to the languid music, talking to her in low tones, telling her just to dance with him. Was it one song, was it three, or five? Time seemed suspended. He muttered her name, his breath stirring her hair, then nothing. And as she moved to his lead she fell deeper into his web.

When the band took a break, she took a moment in the bathroom to try to recover her aplomb—cooling her wrists under the rush of water from the cold tap. She shouldn't have had those shots. She'd barely drunk a drop since, but she felt giddy. And as she looked at her reflection—at her large eyes, and the heightened colour in her cheeks and lips—she knew she didn't want to recover her aplomb at all. She wanted to follow this madness to its natural conclusion. Nothing else seemed to matter any more—nothing but being with Owen. Just for while she was on this fantasy island.

She stepped out of the bathroom and saw him straighten from where he'd been leaning against the wall, eyes trained on her door. She walked over to meet him, but her path was intercepted by Vita, her sister.

'Bella, where have you been all night? More to the point, who is that guy you're dancing with?' Vita looked astounded.

'Owen is an old friend.'

'How old?' The disbelief on her sister's face was mortifying.

'Well, not that old.' Bella looked up to where he stood now looming large and close, right behind Vita, his eyes keen. She just kept slim control of her voice and the hysterical giggle out of it. 'You were born what, about thirty years ago, weren't you?'

'Somewhere thereabouts.' He took the last couple of steps so he stood beside her, circling his arm around her waist as naturally as if he'd done it a thousand times.

Then he smiled at her, a glowing, deeply intimate smile that had Bella blinking as much as Vita. His fingers pressed her slightly closer to him and inside she shook. He held her even more firmly.

When he turned his head to Vita, the smile lost its intimacy but was no less potent. 'You must be Bella's sister, the beautiful bride. Congratulations.'

Vita blinked and took more than a second to recover her manners. 'Thank you…er…Owen. Will we be seeing you tomorrow? You're more than welcome.'

'Well…' he glanced back to Bella and she saw the laugh-

ter dancing in his eyes '…I'd love to be there, but Bella wasn't
sure…'

'Oh, if you're a friend of Bella's, of course you're welcome.'

Bella turned sharply, narrowed her gaze on Vita. Did she
stress the 'if'?

'Thank you.' Owen closed off the conversation smoothly.
And with a nod drew Bella back outside and threaded them
through the dancing couples.

Bella went into his arms hardly thinking about what she
was doing. Melancholy had struck. Vita had seemed stunned
that Bella might actually have a gorgeous guy wanting to be
with her. They were probably all watching agog—amazed at
the development. Oh, why did she have to be here with her
perfect sister and her perfect family—when she was so obviously the odd one out?

He must have read her thoughts because he pulled her
close and looked right in her eyes. 'She's not that perfect.'

She didn't believe him. Her little sister, by a year, had
always been the one to do things how they were supposed to—
the way her father wanted.

'She didn't wish you a happy birthday,' he said softly.

Bella sighed. 'She's preoccupied.' And she was. This wedding was a mammoth operation.

Owen frowned, clearly thinking that it wasn't a good enough
excuse. Warmth flooded her. He was so damn attractive.

'So how many candles should you be blowing out tonight,
Bella?'

'Twenty-four.' She hadn't the energy for joking any more—
she was too focused on her feelings for him. And all of a
sudden the giddiness took over—she couldn't slow the speed
of her heartbeat; her breath was knocked from her lungs. She
stumbled.

His hands tightened on her arms. 'You're tired.'

Tired was the last thing she was feeling.

But he stepped back, breaking their physical contact. 'I'll walk you to your room.'

Disappointment flooded her. She'd been having a wonderful night and she didn't want it to come to an end. But it had—with Vita's interruption the fantasy had been shattered. And Owen was already moving them across the deck, towards the stairs that led to the sandy beach.

She glanced up into his face, hoping for a sign of that glint, only to find it shuttered. Blandly unreadable. The sense of disappointment swelled.

As they reached the steps, Celia stepped in front of them.

'You're not leaving already?' she asked, full of vivaciousness.

'It's a big day tomorrow. Bella needs to turn in now,' Owen answered before she had the chance.

Celia turned her stunning gaze from him to Bella and the glance became stabbing. 'You'd better put some cream on that sunburn or you'll look like a zebra tomorrow.'

Oh, she just had to get that jibe in, didn't she? Bella smarted.

Owen turned slightly. Slowly, carefully, he gave Bella such an intense once-over that she could feel the impact as if he were really touching her, a bold caress. But it was his eyes that kissed—from the tip of her nose all the way to her toes. And then he did touch her. Lifting his hand, with a firm finger, he stroked the red stripe on her chest—from the top of it near her collarbone, down the angled line to where it disappeared into her blouse. His eyes followed the path, and then went lower, seeming to be able to see everything, regardless of the material.

'Don't worry.' He spoke slowly. 'I'll make sure she takes care of it.'

Bella stared up at him, fascinated by the flare in his eyes. The flare that had been there from that moment when she'd turned her head to his voice as she'd sat at the bar. It had flashed now and then as they'd talked and laughed their way through dinner. But now it was back and bigger than before and she couldn't help her response. Every muscle, every fibre, every cell tightened within her. As he looked at her like that, his hunger was obvious to anyone. She'd never felt more wanted than she did in that moment and she was utterly seduced. The whole of his attention was on her and the whole of her responded. But she wasn't just willing, she was wanting.

She dimly heard a cough, but when she finally managed to tear her gaze from his, Celia had already walked off. Bella managed a vague smile after her general direction, but then, compelled by the pull between them, she walked with Owen—barely aware of her cousin's and her sister's gazes following her. She no longer cared. She was too focused on the burn of her skin where his finger had touched, and the excitement burgeoning now as he held her hand and matched her step for step.

CHAPTER FOUR

DOWN on the sand the breeze lifted and the drop in temperature checked Bella.

'Where are you staying?' Owen asked, his voice oddly gentle.

'One of the studios round the back.' She wasn't in one of the luxury villas, but a tiny unit in a building with several other tiny units. It was still nice. It didn't quite have the view and door opening directly onto the beach that the villas did, but it didn't have the price tag either.

'Show me.' Still gentle.

But her mind teased her with what it was that he wanted her to show him. It took only a minute or so to wind around the back of the building, to where the units were. At her door she stopped. She gazed at the frame of it, suddenly shy of wanting to look him in the eye. 'Thank you for seeing me through that.'

'No problem.' He loomed beside her. 'It was fun.'

Fun. Disappointment wafted over her again. Stupid, when he'd given her a victory she'd mentally relive time and time again, but there was something else she wanted now. Something she sensed would be much, much better.

He gestured towards the door. 'Are you alone in there? Not twin sharing with your great-aunt Amelia or anyone awful?'

'All alone. Just me.' She chanced a look up at him then, saw the hint of the smile, the gleam of teeth flashing white in the darkness.

'Want me to come in and make sure there are no monsters in the wardrobe?'

Confidence trickled back through her. She stepped a little closer. 'Quite the gentleman, aren't you? Are you going to turn down my sheet as well?'

'If you like.' He matched her move, stepped closer still. 'Would you like, Bella?'

Such a simple question. It needed only the simplest of answers. And she already knew what he was asking and what her answer would be. There was no way she could ever say no to him. Probably no one had ever said no to him and she didn't blame any of them.

'Yes.'

His head bent. His smile was no wider, but somehow stronger. 'Good.'

His first kiss was soft, just a gentle press of lips on lips. No other contact. Then he pulled away—just a fraction, for just a moment. Then he was back. Another butterfly-light kiss that had her reaching after him when he pulled back again. And as she moved forward he swept her into his arms. Strong and tight they held her and the next kiss changed completely. Deep, then deeper again. The awareness that had sizzled between them all night was unleashed. Her hands threaded through his hair, his hands moulded over her curves. Together they strained closer, lips hungry, tongues tasting. Bella was lost. He felt better than she'd imagined—broad, lean, hard. Her eyes closed as his lips left hers, roving down to her jaw, down her throat, hot and hungry. The fire in her belly roared.

And then he was kissing her sunburn stripe, undoing the top few buttons on her blouse, pulling it open so he could follow the path of reddened skin with lush wet kisses that did anything but soothe. The red stopped on the curve of her breast—where her bikini cup had been. But he didn't stop. He pulled the lace of her bra down until her nipple popped up over it. And then he took that in his mouth too.

She arched back as sensations spasmed deep inside. His other arm took her weight, pulling her pelvis into the heat of his hips, and she could feel his hardness through his jeans. She gasped at the impact—and at the pleasure ricocheting through her system. He lifted his head, his hunger showing in the strain on his face and in his body. The air was cool on her bared skin but she was still steaming up.

Breathless, she pulled back, her blouse hanging half open, breast spilling over her bra. 'I think I better get the door unlocked now.'

'I think you better had,' he teased, but her confidence surged higher when she heard his equal breathlessness. 'Because the thing about sex on the beach,' he added, 'is the sand.'

Giggling, she slipped her hand in her pocket, closed her fingers around the key. Turning, she fumbled to get it into the lock. He stood behind her, ran his hands over her hips and then pressed so close she could feel everything he had to offer. Her hand lurched off course completely. He put his fingers over hers and guided the key safely home.

Pressing even harder against her, he spoke in her ear, hot and full of sexy humour. 'We are having screaming orgasms though, OK?'

'OK.' She just got the door open and the answer out before he spun her around and his mouth came down on hers again. He backed her in, kicking the door shut behind them with his foot. He kept backing her, but angled her direction so after only a couple of paces she was up against the wall. Relief flooded her as she felt it behind her and she half sagged against it. She didn't think her legs were strong enough to hold her up all on their own any more. When the man kissed, all she could think of was a bed, and her desperation to be on it and exploring and feeling and being kissed like that everywhere.

His hands held her face up to his, warm fingers stroked down her neck, but he stood back so his body didn't touch hers. She wanted it to touch again—all of it against her. The kisses grew deeper as she opened more to him—inviting him in with the sighs of pleasure she let escape and the way she sought him with her tongue.

But her confidence came in waves—ebbing again as his caresses became more intimate, as he undid the last buttons and hooks. Shyness overcame her as her blouse and her bra slipped away completely.

He looked down at her, sensing her stillness. 'You're sure?'

She nodded, but explained. 'It's been a while.'

'Me too.'

She didn't believe that for a second. But it was nice of him to say it.

Then her shyness melted as he whisked his shirt over his head and she saw the beauty of his body beneath.

Her hands lifted instinctively, and she spread her fingers on his shoulder, slowly letting them trace down the impressive breadth of his chest and then lower, over the taut upper abs down to where his jeans were fastened. He lifted his head at that, grinning wickedly. 'Stop that, sweetness. It'll all be over all too soon. As it is it's going to be a close one.'

'Very close,' she agreed, letting her fingers walk some more.

'Stop that.' His smile only widened.

'I can't. You feel fantastic. You really do have muscles.' She marvelled at it. How the hell did a computer geek grow muscles like these?

But then her own actions slowed as she became acutely aware of his—of the kisses dulling her sense of initiative. He was taking the lead and increasingly all she could do was follow. Slowly, so slowly, he was stripping the skirt off her. Dropping to his knees, he eased it down, pressing kisses to her thighs and legs.

Then he stood again, him still clad in jeans, her in nothing but knickers. Their shoes had been kicked off somewhere outside the door. He took her face in his hands again, searching her eyes and then smiling. Then kissing. And with every moment of the kiss her need grew. Until, pressing her shoulders against the wall for support, she pushed her hips forward towards him—aching for closeness.

'Something you want?' he asked.

'You know.'

He slid his hands from her shoulders all the way down until he curled his fingers round hers. Then he lifted them, swinging her arms up above her head, pinning them back to the wall with his hands. The movement lifted her breasts, her hard nipples strained straight up to him.

He paused and took advantage of the view. Looking into his eyes, she saw the passion and simply melted more—shivering as she did. Swiftly he kissed her and transferred the possession of both her hands to only one of his. He glided his other hand down her throat, then lower. Cupping her breast, he stroked the taut nipple with his thumb. She whimpered into his mouth. His hand moved again, fingers sliding down her stomach, and then they slipped inside her panties, right down, curving into her, feeling the extent of the warm wetness there as she moaned.

'Mmm.' He lifted his mouth from hers, looked into her eyes as another moan escaped her. And any embarrassment dissolved as she took in his pleased expression.

'That's what I want,' he muttered, kissing her eyes closed, one and then the other. Gentle. His fingers started to work. So slowly, gently. And his mouth pressed to hers again, his tongue exploring, just as his fingers were. Slow and gentle and tormenting. Insistent. And the giddiness was back. She kept her eyes closed, lost in the feeling, utterly at his mercy, until she was writhing and arching and wanting harder and faster. But still he kept it slow, teasing her. And then she was panting, pleading in the scarce moments when he lifted his head to let her take breath.

And he listened, watched, altered his actions. Not so gentle. Faster and deeper. Passionate kisses that bruised her lips and then roved hard over her face and then down. His mouth was hot as he nuzzled his way down the side of her throat, to her breast and back to her starving mouth.

He lifted his head to watch as her panting grew shallower, faster, louder. She started to shake, was begging for him not to stop, for him to give her more.

His eyes gleamed with satisfaction. 'Screaming, remember?'

But he didn't need to tell her. She couldn't stop it anyway, the cry that came as she came—hard and loud.

His fingers loosened on her wrists, her arms dropped down to her sides and he braced his hands on the wall either side of her. He brushed a gentle kiss on her nose.

She shook her head. 'I can't stand any more.'

'Yes, you can.'

'No, I mean literally. I can't stand any more.' And her feet began to slip out in front of her, a slow slither to the floor.

He scooped her straight up.

'Oh, thanks. My legs just didn't want to be upright any more.'

'What do they want?' He chuckled.

'To be wrapped round you. Like this.' She hooked them round his waist and felt her desire for him surge back stronger than before.

'Mmm.' He nodded. 'Feels good to me.'

'Does this feel good?' She slid one hand down his chest, eager to feel his muscles respond.

His arms tightened. 'Thought I told you to quit it.'

'Afraid you can't handle it?'

'Sure am.' His teeth flashed white and she knew he didn't mean it. This guy could handle anything—especially her.

The bed was unmissable and in four paces he had her on it, following immediately. She opened her arms, her mouth, her legs. Ready for everything.

He groaned as he pressed close. 'Condoms?'

She shook her head.

'You don't have any?' He paused and she shook her head again. Then he grinned. 'I do.'

Of course he did. She lay still beneath him as he pulled his wallet out of his back pocket, pulled a small square from inside that and then put it beside her.

'Quite the Boy Scout.'

He met her snark with an unapologetic look. 'Accidents are best avoided, don't you think?'

She nodded. She knew he was right to be prepared—to protect both of them. And then, as he kissed her, she decided his experience was something to celebrate—because nobody had kissed her like this before. No one had known how to turn her on like this. She'd never known such raw lust, or had such an ache for physical fulfilment.

He worked his way down her body, peeling her panties

from her, stoking the fire within with caresses and whispers and kisses. Her hands grappled with the fastening of his jeans—she could wait no longer. But he took over, rolling to his back, tearing the denim from his body and quickly sorting the condom. Then he was back, settling over her, and the level of her anticipation almost had her hyperventilating.

He held back for a second, humour twinkling in the dark desire. 'Happy birthday, Bella.'

She closed her eyes. The first person to actually say it today. And now he was—*oh*! She gasped. Opened her eyes again—wide.

'Birthday girls deserve big presents.' He was watching her closely. 'That OK?'

'Oh, yes.' She squealed as he moved closer and a smile stretched his mouth. Air rushed out from her lungs in jagged segments as her body adjusted to his—to the glorious delight of it.

And then, when she was able to revel in the feel of him, he moved, rolling her over, lifting her so she was sitting astride him while at the same time arching up into her so the connection wasn't lost.

'Let me see how beautiful you are, Bella.'

She looked down at him, marvelling that she was astride such magnificence. His chest tabled out before her and she spread her hands over it, leaning forward so she could slide up his length—and back down. Her eyes closed as she slowly hit his hilt again. And then again and again.

Shuddering, she opened her eyes to see him watching, with his head on the big pillows, appreciation apparent as he roved over her body, taking in her reaction. His hands spread wide, sliding up her thighs, lifting to cup her breasts and then take them in a ripe handful.

'Beautiful Bella,' he muttered, thumbs stroking. His heat fired her to go faster. And then he moved to match her.

'Oh, God,' she gasped. 'You really are a tiger.'

He growled in response.

Her giggle was lost in another gasp as he moved more, encouraging her to take more. And the sensations grew—overwhelming everything. Until there was nothing left in her mind—no thought, no humour, recognition of nothing but this wild passion that was all-consuming. Tension seared through her, until it could tighten no more, making her body rigid as she was thrust to the brink of madness.

His arms encircled her as he surged up with more force and depth than ever, and his hands clenched, supporting her as her orgasm tore through her, taking her strength with it. But he held her hard, making her face the intensity of it, squeezing every last sensation from her until she screamed with the exquisite pleasure of it.

She collapsed forward onto him, his shout still reverberating in her ears. Every muscle quivered—hot and bubbling, seeming to sing and so sensitive she could hardly believe it. She'd never felt anything like it.

'In about half an hour or so,' he murmured as her lids lowered, 'we're going to do that again.'

'And more,' she mumbled. She had plans for him, oh, yes, she had plans...in about half an hour...

There was a strange buzzing sound. As if an oversized bumblebee had made its way in and was trapped inside. Her warm pillow jerked up. Startled, she rolled away, and he quickly slid from the bed. Blinking rapidly so her eyes adjusted, feeling cold, she watched as he found his jeans. He swore crudely as he struggled to find the right pocket in the dark. The screen cast a cold blue glow on his face. He studied it for a moment, then his fingers pressed buttons, fast, frantic.

He glanced up, distance reflected in his eyes. 'What a nightmare.'

She wasn't sure what he was referring to—the message, or the situation. After another minute or so the phone buzzed again. He read the message.

'I have to go,' he said, pushing more buttons.

It wasn't light yet. Not even close. And this was summer in New Zealand when it got light near five a.m. Hell, he was running out in the middle of the night.

'It's so early.'

He had his jeans on and was still pressing buttons. 'In New York, it's nine a.m. and my client needs help right now.'

'But it's Saturday.' He wouldn't even look at her.

'No such thing as Saturdays, not for me. I have to get back right away.'

But what about the wedding? Devastated, she envisaged the hours to come. But she wasn't going to remind him. He'd probably had too much to drink to even remember. The idea of him being her date had only ever been a joke. Except her family knew. Everyone knew. She was on the train to humiliation central.

She drew her knees up. Face it, she was already there. Mortification spread over her skin and she was glad it was dark and her blush hidden. He could hardly wait to leave her. Silently, quickly, he found his top, pulling it over his head. His mind had already left the building.

Frowning at the screen, he spoke. 'Give me your number.'

He was taking the control—not giving her his details, but trying to make her feel better. As if he'd ever call.

'Bella.' He spoke sharply. 'Tell me your number.'

She recited it, with a cold heart and a determined mind.

He nodded, still pressing buttons. 'I'll call you.'

He made it sound sincere. But she knew for a fact he wouldn't.

Thirteen hours and no sleep later, Bella watched Vita and Hamish walk around the beach wearing their cheesy flip-flops that left 'Just Married' imprinted in the sand. She really wished she had a hangover. That way she could blame the whole escapade on booze. Say she'd been blind drunk and shrug the thing off with the insouciance of an ingénue.

But while she was aching, the pain wasn't in her head—it was deep inside her chest and she tried to tell herself it wasn't really that bad. Fact was, she'd never had a one-night stand before. She'd had boyfriends that hadn't lasted long—OK, so all three of her ex-boyfriends would fall into that category. But she'd never had a fling that lasted less than ten hours. And she'd gone and done it in front of her entire family—who thought she was a hopeless case already. What had she been thinking?

And there was Celia, hanging on the arm of Rex, flashing victorious glances her way at every opportunity. Thank goodness he hadn't arrived until this morning and hadn't been witness to last night too. And now everyone was thinking she couldn't hang onto anyone—not the fabulously suitable accountancy star that was Rex or the laid-back, coolly casual sex god that was Owen. Thank heavens her father had spent the night talking business with his brothers—hopefully he wouldn't have heard a thing about it.

She felt a prickle inside as she saw the sheer joy on her sister's face. Maybe Owen had been right—she was a little jealous. But who wouldn't want to be loved like that? And little sister Vita seemed to have it all—she'd been the one to embrace the family profession—as all four of their elder brothers had. Vita had been the one able to do everything the way the family wanted. Even down to marrying one of the partners in the firm. She'd worked really hard to get her degree and her charter. And to cap it off, she was nice. She deserved to be happy.

But Bella worked hard too. Damn hard. Didn't she deserve to be happy? Didn't she deserve some respect too?

She *was* jealous. How nice it would be to have someone look at her the way Hamish looked at Vita. To have the career and the lover. But she'd yet to *get* the job she wanted, and she couldn't even have a one-night stand last the whole night.

As if Owen had really had to get up and go to work at three in the damn morning? On a *Saturday*. He'd probably programmed his phone to buzz then and the talk of the client in New York was just for believability. It was probably his standard modus operandi—enabling him to make that quick escape and avoid the awkward morning-after scene.

The morning after had been unbearably awkward for Bella. And it wasn't just because of the questioning looks of the younger members of the family—the ones who'd been in the restaurant last night. She'd gone to Reception and asked which room 'Owen' was staying in—only to be told there was no Owen staying at all. And no Owen had checked out recently either. Then she'd asked to check her tab, bracing herself for a huge bill from the bar. But she found it had been paid in full, including the accommodation cost. She'd asked whose name was on the card—but apparently whoever it was had paid in cash.

It had been him—she was sure of it. What was he doing— paying for services rendered?

She stood, brushed the sand from the horrendous dress. She wasn't going to sit around and be the object of mockery or pity any more—and certainly not her own self-pity either. It was time for action. Things were going to have to change.

CHAPTER FIVE

A LOT could happen in three weeks and a day. Life-changing decisions could be made and the resulting plans put into action. And it was too late for regrets now. Bella had finally pushed herself out of the nest—and it was time to see if she could fly. Thus far, she was succeeding *barely* on a day-by-day basis.

The minute she'd got back from that hellish weekend she'd moved out of her father's home in Auckland and down to Wellington. Movies were made there. There were theatres. It was the arts hub. She'd found a tiny flat quite easily. Above another flat where a couple lived. It was in the shade of a hill and was a little damp, but it would do. She hadn't wanted to flat-share. She was going independent—all the way.

Because she'd finally had the shove she needed. And it wasn't ambition. It was one humiliation too many. If she ever saw Owen again she'd have to thank him. His was the boot that had got her moving. The smug sideways glances of Celia, the questions in her perfect sister's eyes at the reception. Bella had explained that he'd had to leave for work. It had sounded lame even to her. When they'd asked what he did, where he worked, she'd only been able to parrot the vague answers that he'd given her.

She didn't want to run the risk of bumping into him ever

again. It would have been just her luck that he'd have come into the café where she'd worked in central Auckland.

So now she worked at a café in central Wellington. The manager of that branch of the chain had jumped at the chance to hire someone already trained, and with so much experience she could step in as deputy manager any time he needed. And she'd started children's party entertaining here too. She'd had a couple of recommendations from contacts in Auckland and today's supreme effort had ensured a booking for her second party already. Several other parents had asked for her card at the end of it too. It wasn't exactly glam work, but she was good at it.

But then there was the lecherous uncle. There was always one. The younger brother of the mother, or the cousin of the father, who fancied a woman in a fairy dress. He'd cornered her as she was packing up her gear.

'Make *my* wish come true. Have dinner with me.'

As if she hadn't heard that one before. Then he'd touched her, an attempt at playfulness. He'd run his fingers down her arm and they'd felt reptilian. She'd made a quick exit—smiling politely at the hosts. Once out the door she'd bolted, because she'd seen him coming down the hall after her. She'd been in such a hurry to get into the car and away she'd pulled hard on her dress as she'd sat and one of the cute capped sleeves had just ripped right off, meaning that side of the top was in imminent danger of slipping south too. Well, the dress had been slightly tight. She'd been eating a little more choco- late than usual these last three weeks. Like a couple of king-size cakes a day to get her through the move. Now she needed to top up on essential supplies. And so it was that she pulled into the supermarket car park—fully costumed up and half falling out of it.

Ordinarily she'd never stop and shop while in character, but this wasn't an ordinary day. She was tired and ever so slightly depressed. She picked up a basket on her way in and ignored the looks from the other customers. Didn't they often see fully grown women wearing silver fairy dresses and wings, an eyeload of make-up and an entire tube of glitter gel?

She'd blow her last fifteen dollars on some serious comfort food. She loaded in her favourite chocolate. The best ice cream—she could just afford the two-litre pack so long as she could find a five-dollar bottle of wine. In this, one of the posher supermarkets, she might be pushing her luck. As it was her luck was always limited.

She headed to the wine aisle and searched for the bright yellow 'on special' tags. She'd just selected one particularly dodgy-looking one when the voice in her ear startled her.

'And you told me you didn't want the fluffy princess part.'

Her fingers were around the wine, taking the weight, but at the sound of that smooth drawl they instinctively flexed.

The bottle smashed all over the floor—wine splattered everywhere, punctuated by large shards of green glass.

Oh, great. It would have to happen to her. Right this very second. She looked hard at the rapidly spreading red puddle on the floor so she wouldn't have to face the stares of the gazillion other customers, especially not... Was it really him?

'Sorry, I didn't mean to give you such a fright.'

She couldn't avoid it any longer. She looked up at—yes, it was him. Right there. Right in front of her. And utterly devastating.

'Oh, no.' The words were out before she thought better of it. 'What are *you* doing here? I thought you lived in—' She broke off. Actually she had no idea where he lived. She'd thought Auckland, but there was no real reason for her to have done so. They hadn't really talked details much—not about anything that really mattered.

After a disturbingly stern appraisal, he bent, picked up the fragment of wine bottle and read the smeared label. It reminded her where they were and the mess she'd just made. She glanced down the aisle and saw a uniform-clad spotty teenager headed their way with a bucket and mop.

'No, no, no and no again.' Owen, if that indeed was his name, was shaking his head.

'It's for cooking. A casserole.' Ultra defensive, she invented wildly.

He drew back up to full height and looked in her basket. Both brows flipped. 'Some casserole.'

'It is actually,' she breezed, determined to ignore the heat in her cheeks. 'Pretty extraordinary.'

'Ultra extraordinary,' he said, still looking at her with a sharpness that was making her feel guilty somehow. It maddened her—he was the one who'd skipped out that crazy night. Don't think about it. Do *not* think about it!

But suddenly it was all back in a rush—all she could see was him naked, her body remembering the warmth of his, the thrill. And all she could hear was his low laughter and how seductive it had been.

The heat in her cheeks went from merely hot to scorching. And he stood still and watched its progression—degree, by slow degree.

Then his gaze dropped, flared and only then did she remember the state of her dress. Quickly she tugged the low sagging neckline up and kept her fist curled round the material just below her shoulder.

His eyes seemed to stroke her skin. 'Your sunburn has faded.'

It didn't feel as if it had now—it felt more on fire than it had weeks ago when it had been almost raw.

'I'm sorry about this.' He gestured to the mess. 'I'll pay for it.'

And then she remembered how he'd left her.

'No, thanks,' she said briskly. 'You don't have to—'

He wasn't listening. He'd turned, studying the shelves of wine. After a moment he picked one out and put it in her basket. 'I think this one will serve you better.'

She caught a glimpse of a white tag—not a yellow 'on special' one—and winced. No way could she afford that bottle of wine. But she couldn't put it back in front of him.

Then he took her basket off her. 'Is that everything you need for your casserole?' he asked blandly.

'Oh, er, sure.'

He turned away from her and headed towards the check-out. She paused, staring after him, panic rising. More humilia-tion was imminent. She'd chopped up her credit card—not wanting to get into debt—so all she had was that fifteen dollars in her pocket. While she had the cheque from the birthday party she'd just done, it was Sunday and she couldn't cash it.

And no way was she letting him pay her bill—not *again*.

But he put both lots of shopping on the conveyor belt. His was all connoisseur—prime beef steak, a bag of baby spinach, two bottles of hellishly expensive red wine. She couldn't help wondering if he was cooking for a date. Then, as she help-lessly watched, he paid for it all—hers as well as his—with a couple of crisp hundred-dollar bills.

Cash. Of course. But as he put the change back in his wallet, she saw the array of cards in there too—exclusive, private banking ones—and she really started to seethe.

* * *

Owen didn't glance her way once during the transaction. He tried to focus on getting the shopping sorted, but all the while his mind was screening the sight of her spilling out of that un-believable dress.

Bella Cotton. The woman who'd haunted his dreams every night for the last three weeks. He was mad with her. Madder with himself for not being able to shake her from his head.

And now here she was—real and in the beautifully round flesh he couldn't help but remember. She didn't exactly seem thrilled to see him. In fact she looked extremely uncomfort-able. Well, so she should, after fobbing him off with a false number like that.

But her embarrassment only made him that bit madder. Made him feel perverse enough to drag out their bumping into each other even longer. Made him all the more determined to interfere and help her out because she so clearly didn't want him to. How awful for her to have to suffer his company for a few more minutes. He very nearly ground his teeth.

Well, he hadn't wanted her to take up as much of his brain space as she had these last few weeks either. Night after night, restless, he'd thought of her—suffered cold showers because of her. During the day too—at those quiet moments when he should have been thinking of important things. He'd even got so distracted one day he'd actually searched for her on the Internet like some sad jilted lover.

So he'd known she was in Wellington, but he hadn't known where or why or for how long. He certainly hadn't expected to see her in his local supermarket. And he sure as hell hadn't expected her to be wearing the most ridiculous get-up—or half wearing it. And he most definitely hadn't expected to feel that rush of desire again—because he was mad with her, wasn't he? He *was* that jilted lover. He really wanted to know why she'd done it—why when even now, for a few moments, he'd seen that passionate rush reflected in her eyes.

So while the rational part of him was telling him to hand over her shopping and walk away asap, the wounded-male-pride bit was making him hold onto it. The flick of desire was making sure his grip was tight.

He was walking out of the supermarket already. Hadn't looked at her once while at the checkout—not even to ask whether it was OK with her. He'd just paid for the lot, ensured their goods were separately bagged and then picked them up. Now he was carrying both sets of shopping out to the car park. She had no option but to follow behind him—her temper spiking higher with every step. And seeing him still looking so hot, casual in jeans and tee again, made every 'take me' hormone start jiggling inside. She stopped them with an iron-hard clench of her teeth and her tummy muscles. She was angry with him. He'd done a runner and insulted her with his payment choices.

But she could hardly wrench the bag off him. Not in front of everyone—she was already causing a big enough scene.

Her car was parked in the first row. She stopped beside it and sent a quick look in his direction to assess his reaction. He was looking at it with his bland-man expression. It only made her even more defensive.

'She's called Bubbles. The kids like it.'

'Kids?'

'I'm a children's party entertainer. The fairy.' People usually laughed. It wasn't exactly seen as the ultimate work and as a result her credibility—especially with her family—was low. They thought it was the biggest waste of her time ever.

He nodded slowly. 'Hence the wings.'

'And the frock.'

There was a silence. 'Do you do adult parties?'

'That's the third time I've been asked that today,' she snapped. 'You're about to get the non-polite answer.'

His grin flashed for the first time. And she was almost floored once more. Or she would have been if she weren't feeling so cross with him—Mr I'll-Pay-For-Everything-Including-You.

Her ancient Bambini was painted baby-blue and had bright-coloured spots all over it. She quickly unlocked it, glancing pointedly at the bag he was carrying, not looking higher than his hand.

Silently he handed it over. 'Thanks.' She aimed for blitheness over bitterness but wasn't entirely sure of her success. 'Nice to see you again.' Saccharine all over. She got in the car before she lost it, ending the conversation, and hitting the ignition.

Nothing.

She tried again. Willed the car to start. Start before she made even more of an idiot of herself.

The engine choked. Her heart sank. Had the long drive down from Auckland finally done the old darling in? She tried the ignition once more. It choked again.

He knocked on the window. Reluctantly she wound it down.

'Having trouble?'

She wasn't looking at him. She was looking at the fuel gauge. The arrow was on the wrong side of E. Totally on the wrong side. It was beyond the red bit and into the nothing. As in NOTHING. No petrol. Nada. Zip.

Man, she was an idiot. But relief trickled through her all the same. She had real affection for the car she'd had for years and had painted herself.

She took a deep breath. She could fake it, right? At least

try to get through the next two minutes with a scrap of dignity? She got out of the car.

'Problem?'

Did he have to be so smooth? So calm, so damn well in control? Didn't he do dumb things on occasion?

'I forgot something,' she answered briefly. Now she remembered the warning light had been on—when was that? Yesterday? The day before? But it had gone off. She'd thought it was OK, that it had been a warning and then changed its mind. She mentally gave herself a clunk in the head—as if it had found some more petrol in its back pocket?

Clearly not. It had completely run out of juice. And the nearest garage was... Where was it exactly? The only one she could think of was the one near her flat—the one she should have filled up at this morning, had she had the funds.

'What?' he asked—dry, almost bored-sounding.

But she was extremely conscious that he hadn't taken his eyes off her. And she was doing everything not to have to look into them, because they were that brilliant blue and she knew how well they could mesmerise her.

She tugged her top up again. 'Petrol.'

'Oh.' He looked away from her then, seeming to take an age looking at the other cars. She realised he was barely holding in his amusement. Finally he spoke. 'The nearest service station is just—'

'Uh, no, thanks,' she interrupted. 'I'll go home first.'

There was no way she was having him beside her when she put five dollars into a jerry can so she could cough and splutter the car home and leave it there until her cheque cleared. After this final splurge it was going to be a tin of baked beans and stale bread for a couple of days. No bad thing given the way she was spilling out the top of the fairy frock.

'How far away is home?'

'Not far.' A twenty-minute walk. Make that thirty in her sequined, patent leather slippers.

There was a silence. She felt his gaze rake her from head to toes—lingering around the middle before settling back up on her face. Heat filled her and she just knew he was enjoying watching her blush deepen. She stared fixedly at the seam on the neckline of his tee shirt and refused to think of anything but how much she was going to appreciate her ice cream when she got the chance.

And then he asked, 'Can I give you a ride?' Mockery twisted his lips, coloured the question and vexed her all the more.

Get a ride with him? Oh, no. She'd already had one ride of sorts and that was plenty, right? She could cope with this just fine on her own.

She'd call the breakdown service. But then she remembered it was her father's account and she refused to lean on him again. Independence was her new mantra. They wouldn't take her seriously until she got herself sorted. Until she proved she was completely capable of succeeding alone. She frowned; she'd have to walk.

'You trusted me enough to sleep with me, I think you can trust me to run you home safely.'

She looked straight at him then, taken by his soft words. With unwavering intensity, he regarded her. She'd known she'd be stunned if she looked into his eyes—brilliant, blue and beautiful. Good grief, he was gorgeous. So gorgeous and all she could think about was how great he'd felt up close and every cell suddenly yearned for the impact.

Her own eyes widened as she read his deepening expression—was there actually a touch of chagrin there? Why?

'Thanks.' It was a whisper. It wasn't what she'd meant to say at all.

* * *

His car sat low to the ground, gleaming black and ultra expensive. The little badge on the bonnet told her that with its yellow background and rearing black horse. He unlocked it, opened the door. She started as the door and seemingly half the roof swung up into the air.

She sent a sarcastic look in his direction. 'That's ridiculous.'

'No, Bella, *that's* ridiculous,' he said, pointing back to her Bambini.

She bent low and managed to slide in without popping right out of her top. The interior was polished and smooth and impeccably tidy and also surprisingly spartan. She tried to convince herself the seat wasn't that much more comfortable than the one in her own old banger. But it was—sleek and moulding to her body.

Owen took the driver's seat, started the engine—a low growl. 'He's called Enzo.'

'I'd have thought it would be more plush.'

He shook his head. 'It's the closest thing to a Formula One racing car you can drive on conventional streets.'

'Oh.' Like that was fabulous?

Her feigned lack of interest didn't stop him. 'I like things that go fast.'

She looked at him sharply. He was staring straight ahead, but his grin was sly and it was widening with every second.

Coolly as she could, she gave him her address. The sooner she got home and away from him, the sooner she could forget about it all and get on with her new life.

The fire vehicle outside her house should have warned her—nothing ever went smoothly for Bella. There was always some weird catastrophe that occurred—the kind of thing that was so outrageous it would never happen to other normal people.

Like being caught in a ripped fairy dress in the supermarket by her only one-night stand—the guy who'd given her the best sexual experience of her life.

'Looks like there might be some kind of trouble.' He stated the obvious calmly as he parked the car.

She stared at the big red appliance with an impending sense of doom intuitively knowing it was something to do with her. She'd have done something stupid. But behind the truck, the house still stood. She released the breath she'd been holding.

'I'm sure whatever's happened isn't that major.'

So he figured it had something to do with her too. She might as well walk around with a neon sign saying 'danger, accident-prone idiot approaching'. But her embarrassment over everything to do with him faded into the background as she got out of the car and focused on whatever had gone wrong now.

As she walked up the path, one seriously bad smell hit her. The couple from the downstairs flat were standing in the middle of the lawn. A few firemen were standing next to them talking. Silence descended as she approached, but they weren't even trying to hide their grins. It was a moment before she remembered her fairy dress and quickly put her hand to her chest. Wow, what an entrance.

'You left something on the hob.' The head fire guy stepped forward.

She'd what?

'I think you were hard-boiling some eggs.'

Oh, hell—she had been, the rest of the box because they'd been getting dangerously close to their use-by date and she hadn't wanted to waste any. She'd decided to cook them up and have them ready for the next day, and then in the rush to get to the café and pack all her party gear, she'd forgotten all about them.

Isla, her neighbour, piped up, 'They had to break down the door—we didn't have a key.'

The doors to both flats were narrow and side by side. Only now hers was smashed—splinters of wood lay on the ground, and the remainder of the door was half off its hinges.

'I'm so sorry,' she mumbled.

She trudged up the stairs and almost had a heart attack when she saw the damage to the door up there too. The whole thing would have to be replaced as well as the one downstairs. Bye bye bond money. And she'd probably be working extra hours at the café to make up the rest of it.

She stared around at the little room she'd called home for a grand total of two weeks. Her first independent, solely occupied home. There was almost no furniture—a beanbag she liked to curl into and read a book or watch telly. But it had been hers. Now it was tainted by the most horrendous smell imaginable and she couldn't imagine it ever being a welcome sanctuary again. She'd spoilt things—again—with her own stupidity.

'You can't stay here.'

She nearly jumped out of her skin when Owen spoke.

'No.' For one thing the smell was too awful. For another it was no longer secure with both doors broken like that. She wouldn't sleep a wink.

She saw him looking around, figured he must be thinking how austere it was. When his gaze came to rest on her again, concern was evident in his eyes. She didn't much like that look. She wasn't some dippy puppy that needed to be taken care of.

'Can I drop you somewhere else?'

Her heart sank even lower into her shiny slippers. The last thing she wanted to do was call on the family. Having finally broken out she wanted to manage—for more than a month at least. If she phoned them now she'd never get any credibility. The two months' deposit on the flat had taken out her savings, but she didn't care. She'd wanted to be alone, to be independent, and she'd really wanted it to work this time. She could check into a hostel, but she had no money. She had nowhere to go. She'd have to stay here, put a peg on her nose and her ear on the door.

He took a step in her direction. 'I have a spare room at my place.'

She looked at him—this stranger whom she knew so intimately, yet barely knew at all.

'Grab a bag and we'll get out of here. Leave it and come back tomorrow.' He spoke lightly. 'It won't be nearly so bad then.'

She knew it was a good idea but she felt sickened. It was the last straw on a hellish day and her slim control snapped. Anger surged as she stared at him. Irrationally she felt as if he were to blame for everything. 'Is your name really Owen?'

He looked astonished. 'Of course. Why do you ask?'

'I asked at the hotel reception for you.' She was too stewed to care about what that admission might reveal. 'They had no record of any Owen staying there.'

He paused, looked a touch uncomfortable. 'I wasn't staying at the resort.'

She stared at him in disbelief.

'I have a holiday house just down from it.'

A holiday house—in one of the most exclusive stretches of beach on Waiheke Island? Who the hell was he?

He looked away, walked to the window. 'No strings, Bella,' he said carelessly, returning to her present predicament. 'All

I'm offering is a place to stay for a couple of days until this mess gets cleaned up.'

Bella pushed the memories out and internally debated. She didn't have much in the way of personal possessions—nothing of any great value anyway. The most important stuff was her kit for the parties and that was in her car. It wouldn't take five minutes to chuck a few things into a bag. And maybe, if she took up his offer, she could keep this latest catastrophe to herself? Her family need never know.

Slowly, she swallowed her remaining smidge of pride. 'Are you sure?'

'Of course.' He shrugged, as if it was nothing. It probably was nothing to him. 'I work all hours. I'll hardly notice you're there.'

She knew she could trust him; he certainly didn't seem as if he was about to pounce. He'd gone running away in the night, hadn't he? Humiliation washed over her again. But she had little choice—her family or him. She picked him—she'd lost all dignity as far as he was concerned already. Maybe she could keep the scrap she had left for her father. 'OK.'

Owen failed to hide his smile, so turned quickly, heading down the stairs to deal with the fire crew. He fixed the bottom door enough to make it look as all right as possible from the outside and gave a half-guilty mutter of thanks for her misfortune. He wasn't afraid to take advantage of this situation—not when she'd so coolly cut him loose that night. Because that flick of desire had blown to full-on inferno again—from a mere five minutes in her company. And now he had the perfect opportunity to have even more of her company—one night, maybe two. Enough to find out what had gone wrong, and then to finish what had started.

Bella stuffed a few clothes into a bag—not many—while dwelling on the glimpse of that wide, wicked, Waiheke smile he'd just flashed. It would only be one night. Two, tops.

Not taking sexy black lingerie. *Not* taking sexy black lingerie.

Somehow it ended up stuffed at the bottom of the bag.

CHAPTER SIX

THINGS came in threes, right? And Bella had had her three—her dress, the wine and now her flat. Surely nothing else could go wrong with this day?

'Is there anyone you should call?' Owen asked, opening the car door for her.

She shook her head. 'I'll take care of it later.'

'Then let's go.'

She sat back and tried to relax as he turned the car round and headed back towards the centre of town. He slowed as they hit what had once been the industrial district with lots of warehouses for storing the goods that came in on the harbour. Only now most of the warehouses had been converted—restaurants, upmarket shops and residential conversions in the upper storeys. It was the ultimate in inner-city living with theatres around the corner, Te Papa the national museum, the best film house in the country and shops, shops, shops. All less than a five-minute walk away.

He pulled in front of one warehouse. On one side of it was a restaurant, the other a funky design store. But there was nothing in the ground floor of this one. The windows were darkened. His car window slid down and he reached out to press numbers of the security pad that stood on a stand in front. The wide door opened up and he drove the car in. In the dim light she saw a big empty space—save for a mountain bike and some assorted gym equipment. It immediately reminded her of his muscles. She looked away. There was a lift to the side and a steep flight of stairs heading up in a straight line. He stepped forward, tackling the stairs.

'My apartment is on the top floor.'

Of course it was. On the third level there was another security pad, another pin number. The guy was clearly security conscious. Once inside she blinked—her eyes taking a second to cope with the transition from gloomy stairwell to bright room. It was huge. At first glance all she saw were wooden floors, bricks, steel beams. Half the roof had been ripped off and replaced with skylights—flooding the place in fresh, natural light. There was a huge table in the centre, surrounded by an assortment of chairs, but it was the long workbench that ran the length of one wall that caught her attention.

'Is your computer screen big enough?' She stared in amazement at the display of technology lined up on it. 'Have you got enough of them?'

He grinned. 'Actually most of them are in the office on the second floor.'

'So what, these are just for fun?'

He gave her a whisker of a wink, a faint fingerprint of the humour he'd had that night on Waiheke. Then it was gone. He walked ahead of her, leading her to the kitchen area, and she watched awkwardly as he put items into the fridge and freezer.

'Most of the apartment has yet to be done. After getting my room and the kitchen done I just ran out of—'

'Money?' she interpolated hopefully. Surely she couldn't have been so far wrong about this guy.

'Time,' he corrected, smiling faintly. 'Business has been

busy.' He looked about. 'The basic design is there but I haven't had the chance to get the last bits done yet.' He glanced at her. 'I'll show you to your room.'

It was on the far side of the living area. There were more rooms heading down the corridor next to it, but through their open doors she could see that they were empty. In the room he stopped at, there was just a bed and a chest of drawers.

'Sorry it's so bare.'

She shook her head. 'I'm used to less.'

'I'll make up the bed.'

'I can do it.' She didn't want him in the room any more than necessary.

She took a look out the window—it overlooked the street; she could see all the shoppers. There was a seriously yummy smell wafting up from the Malaysian restaurant next door. 'You must eat out all the time.'

He answered from the doorway. 'They do me take-out packages. But I try to cook a few nights a week. The downside is the rubbish collection—before six o'clock every morning all the bottles from the night before get tipped into the recycling truck. Makes a hell of a din.'

'I'd have thought you'd be well up by then anyway.' She shot him a look. *'Working.'*

That hint of humour resurged, warming her. It was then she fully recognised the danger—she was still hopelessly attracted to him. If he turned on the smile charm again she'd be his in a heartbeat.

She kicked herself. He wasn't offering anything but a room, remember? And she didn't want his sort of gratitude. Tiredness swamped her and the fairy dress slipped lower. She desperately needed a shower. Desperately needed to get dressed in something far more concealing. 'Do you mind if I use the bathroom?'

The amusement in his eyes became unholy. 'Sure. Follow me.'

He led her back into the main space, and across it. Her footsteps slowed as she spied what was through the doorway he was headed to—a very big bed with most definitely masculine-coloured coverings.

'We'll have to share the bathroom—is that OK?'

'Um…sure,' she mumbled. 'That's fine.'

She was in his bedroom. Her skin was prickling with heat.

'The bathroom is one of the things yet to be finished.' He was talking again. 'There's a loo near the kitchen, but the only shower and bath at the moment are the ones in the en suite for the master bedroom.'

The master bedroom—his bedroom—*this* bedroom. Oh, life couldn't be so cruel.

He was watching her with that wicked twinkle faintly sparking in his eyes. 'It's a really nice shower.'

She was quite sure it would be. She wanted to ask if there was a lock on the door, but thought better of being so rude. She hurriedly looked away from him, only to get an eyeful of his walk-in wardrobe space—and all the suits that were hanging there.

Suits.

Completely thrown, she followed where he'd wandered into the bathroom. It was her turn to stop in the doorway.

He stood in the centre of the room. He turned towards her, his smile satisfied. 'It's something, isn't it?'

She nodded. It was all she could manage.

'When I get the chance I'll get the rest of place up to standard too.'

It was beautiful. A huge wet play area that oozed with refined elegance. All the fittings were obviously expensive. The colourings were muted—dark grey, black with sparse splashes of red. A shower space with ample room for two and the biggest bath she'd ever seen.

She railed against her own appreciation of it. Materialistic was not her—there were other, more important things in life. And yet there was no way she couldn't indulge in such classical luxury. No way she couldn't stop thinking of him in there too.

'Take as long as you want,' he said, passing her so closely she shivered. 'You'll find everything you need in here.'

She sagged against the door after he closed it behind him. What she wanted and needed had just walked out.

The kitten heels of her slippers echoed on the wooden floors as she walked back through to the kitchen. She could smell the most delicious smell. So good it wiped the final traces of the rank burnt-egg odour from her senses.

He was barefoot and looking like that careless, gorgeous hunk of a guy she'd met that wild night. Again she was transported back to the moments when she'd felt the firmness of his denim-wrapped thighs between hers. When he'd pulled her close on the dance floor, even closer in her room… Somewhere inside she softened…and immediately she sought to firm up again.

This was the guy who'd been so keen to get away he'd sneaked out in the crazy hours.

This was the guy who wasn't anything like she'd thought, who'd totally misled her—hadn't he?

Now he was standing in his designer kitchen stirring something in a wok with a quick hand. She hovered near the edge of the bench and watched as he added the now diced beef into the mix. Another pot was on the hob and, judging from the steam rising, was on rapid boil.

He glanced up at her. 'You must be hungry.'

Yes, her mouth was definitely watering. And it wasn't the only part of her growing damper. She shifted further away from him. 'How many?'

'How many what?'

'How many are coming to dinner? You could feed an army with a steak that size.'

'Just me.' He laughed. 'And now you.'

'You really are a tiger,' she murmured, turning to look at the living area again, not really meaning for him to hear. 'So your office is on the level downstairs?' She tried to go for some safe conversation.

'Yeah,' he answered. 'I'm not sure what I want to do with the ground-floor level yet. Not a restaurant, that's for sure. Maybe retail?' He shrugged.

He could afford to leave it untenanted? Inner-city space like this would be worth a fortune. *He* must be worth a fortune. Her heart sank lower.

How could she have been so wrong? Stupid. Most women would be thrilled to discover someone was actually a kazillionaire. But it just emphasised to Bella her lack of judgment—and the fact she was so out of place here. She'd never be the girl for anyone as successful as this; she was too much of a liability, too much of a joke. Moodily she stared at the dream space again.

But like a bee to honey she was drawn to look back, watching as he poured in an unlabelled jar of the something that smelt heavenly. Intrigued, she couldn't not ask. 'What's that?'

His wicked look was back. 'The restaurant down the road gives it to me on the sly.'

'It smells incredible.'

'And that's nothing on how it tastes.' He nodded to a

slimline drawer. 'You'll find cutlery in there. Put some on that tray, will you?'

She was glad for something to do. It meant she had to turn her back on him and not watch the impressive cook on display.

'So how long have you been living in that flat?' he called to her above the sizzling sound of the searing meat.

'Two weeks.'

'Really?' He'd moved so he could see her and she could see the lift of his brows.

'I've only just moved to Wellington.'

'Why the shift?'

'To further my career.' The wedding had been the catalyst. The last push she'd needed to finally get out of there and turn her dreams to reality. Only, already it was falling apart.

'Oh?'

'There are good theatres here. The movie industry is based here.'

'There are good cafés here,' he added, full of irony.

She tossed her head. 'There are.'

'So why now?' He was putting food on plates and she was so hungry she could hardly concentrate on what she was saying.

'It needed to happen.'

'You've got work already?'

She nodded and admitted it. 'I've got a job at one of those good cafés. And I'm going to hit the audition circuit.' She'd already scoped the talent agencies. Knew which ones she was going to target. Hopefully they'd take her on. And then it was a matter of keeping trying and hoping for Lady Luck to smile on her.

He lifted the plates onto the tray. Noodles with wilted spinach and slices of seared beef. Her mouth watered. She hadn't had a meal as good as this in weeks.

'Wine?'

She hadn't noticed the bottle of red standing on the bench. 'Thanks.'

He added the bottle to the tray, glanced at her, all irony again. 'Can you manage the glasses?'

'I think so,' she answered coolly.

She followed him up the stairs she hadn't even noticed earlier. They literally climbed to the roof—to a door that took them right out onto it.

The air outside was warm and not too windy. Most of the roof was bare, but there was a collection of plants in pots lined up close together. As he led her around them she saw they created a hedge. On the sheltered side a small table stood, with a couple of chairs, and a collection of smaller pots holding herbs, a couple holding cherry-tomato bushes. It wasn't a huge garden, but it was well cared for. And the view took in the vibrant part of the city, gave them a soundtrack that was full of life.

He balanced the tray on the edge of the table, unloaded the plates with such ease she knew he'd done it countless times before. Just how many women had dined on his roof? It was, she speculated, the perfect scene for seduction.

Well, not hers. Not again.

But she sat when he gestured and he sat too. He seemed bigger than she recalled. His legs were close under the table and it would be nothing to stretch out and brush hers against his. She felt the flush rise in her cheeks and took a sip of the wine so she could hide behind the glass.

'I've organised for your car to be taken to my local garage. I'll get them to check the tyres too. A couple looked a little bald.'

Bella's nerves jangled. The wine tasted sharper. She swallowed it down hard. She couldn't afford new tyres and the last thing she wanted to be was even more indebted to him. A night in his spare room she could deal with. But nothing more. And fixing up her car was well beyond her at the moment. She didn't want to be dependent on anyone. Certainly didn't want to be beholden to him.

'I'd really prefer that you didn't,' she said with as much dignity as she could muster. 'I can take care of it myself.'

And she would. She was over having people interfering and trying to organise her life for her, as if they all thought she couldn't. As if they thought the decisions she made were ill judged.

He didn't reply immediately—coolly having a sip of his wine and seeming to savour it while studying her expression. 'At least let me arrange to have it brought here. It'll be a sitting duck left in a supermarket car park like that.'

She bit the inside of her lip. He was right. It was the ideal target for teenage joyriders—irresistible, in fact. And she loved Bubbles, would hate to see her wrecked, which she would be if any boy racers decided to have a laugh in her. Besides, she suddenly remembered all her party gear was in the back. She certainly couldn't afford to replace all that in a hurry. She knew that once again she couldn't refuse him.

'OK,' she capitulated in a low voice. 'Thanks.'

She sampled some of her dinner. He was right, the sauce was divine—and so was the way he'd cooked the meat in it. But she couldn't enjoy it as much as she ought—the day's events were catching up with her and she realised just what the small fire in her flat had meant. The silence grew and while she knew she should make the attempt she couldn't think what to say. It was like the white elephant in the room—that subject she was determined to avoid. How did people play this sort of thing? How would some sophisticate handle it? How did she pretend bumping into the guy she'd had the hottest sex of her life with was no big deal? But it was a big deal.

Because she wanted it again—badly. Only he'd walked away so quickly, so easily and seemingly without thought to where it had left her.

And now, seeing him in his home environment, she knew he was nothing like the guy she'd pegged him as. He was way out of her league and, judging by the blandly polite way he was dealing with her, he was no longer interested anyway.

He rested his fork on his plate and looked at her. 'So tell me about the wedding.'

She lowered her fork too. So he did remember about that—did he remember he'd offered to be her date too? She shrugged the question off. 'What's to tell?'

Owen lifted his fork again and determinedly focused on his food. It was just like that night on Waiheke—one glance and all he wanted to do was take her to bed. For that time in the bar he couldn't have cared less about work and the commitments he knew were burdening him. Not until he'd had her. But then those commitments had pulled. He'd cursed it at the time, mentally swearing as he'd worked through the early hours answering the questions his client had been struggling with.

He'd walked from her. He'd had to work—that was his first priority. It was the one thing he knew he could be relied on to do, and all the while he'd been doing it he'd been thinking of her—of the most spectacular sex of his life. But then, only a few hours later, he'd tried her number, wanting to apologise for letting her down about the wedding and for walking out so fast, but found it rang to someone who'd never heard of her.

Stung, he'd decided it was for the best—a one-off, as most

of his encounters were. It was the way he liked it—simple, uncomplicated, with no threat of someone wanting something more from him, emotionally or financially. He'd been appalled to discover years ago that he didn't have the 'more' emotionally to give. When Liz had tried to force a commitment, he'd realised damn quick how much he didn't want the burden of it. He couldn't meet high needs, high maintenance, high anything. He didn't want the responsibility of family and forever and all that. Casual, brief, fun. That was all he offered and all he wanted.

But it still niggled. She'd cut at his pride. Tony's Lawn Mowing Service. He wouldn't forget that low point in a hurry.

'Was it fun?' He wanted to see if she'd refer to it. Would she even apologise? But instead she was looking at him as if he were the one who had something to be sorry about. Well, he didn't think so.

But he didn't want to challenge her—not yet. He'd bide his time—see if the sizzle was still there for her as it was for him. Because if it was, and he was pretty sure it was, then he wanted to rouse it. He wanted her wanting him again—and not hiding it. That would be the moment to strike. And once he'd heard her reason, had her apology, he'd have her.

He figured it couldn't be as good again—it had been a unique set of circumstances leading to that explosion between them on Waiheke. Sex that good definitely wasn't possible a second time—it would be fun, but it would be finished. Maybe then he'd get some sleep again.

'The wedding was nice.' She spoke in a resigned voice. 'Beautiful food, fabulous setting.'

And a beautiful bridesmaid—he knew that for a fact. 'And the company?'

Her smile was filled with rue. 'Was as expected.'

'You didn't enjoy it.'

She screwed up her face. 'Not parts of it, no. But some things were great.'

'Your family approves of the groom?' He got the impression family approval was something of a major in Bella's life.

'Oh, yes.' The answer came quickly. 'Hamish is a nice guy. He loves Vita. He makes her happy. But that's not why Dad was so happy to have him marry her.'

'No?' He couldn't stop the questions, found he was more and more intrigued as her face grew even more expressive.

She rolled her eyes. 'Money. It all comes down to doing the maths and in the spreadsheet Hamish has it all. He has the right job and went to the right school. Drives the right car, lives in the right suburb. That's the measure. Visible, measurable success.'

Success, huh? He thought of her tiny unfurnished flat, her barely road-safe car, the bad budget wine she'd been about to buy. He felt a twinge of sympathy for her father. 'Maybe he just wants security for her.'

'What sort of security?' she scoffed. 'It wouldn't matter to him if he was a complete jerk, so long as he could check the right boxes he'd be happy.'

He sensed the hurt in her again. Figured he knew its source. 'Let me guess—you had a boyfriend who didn't measure up.'

'Actually, no. He was exactly what my father wanted.'

A crazy spurt of competition flared through him. 'How so?'

'He had it all.' She ticked off her fingers. 'An accountant. Very successful. Has the car, the apartment. Really good at team sports, the works. The whole family loved him.'

'So what went wrong?'

'He wanted me to wear something more conservative.'

Owen stared at her, only just holding back the burst of laughter. He couldn't imagine Bella allowing that in a million years. Not this woman who was currently wearing some huge flowing blouse and a skirt that was so long it practically dragged on the ground. And he was spending far too long mentally pushing the whole ugly lot off her.

She stared at him, all defiance. 'Nobody tells me what I should or shouldn't wear.'

'That was it?' he asked.

'That was just the start.' She stabbed another bite of meat. 'I'm not interested in someone who wants to change me. Or who wants me to be something I'm not.'

Fair enough point. And he was pleased he'd been right. The guy must have been blind to not see how expression of her individuality was a cornerstone for Bella. 'So what happened to him?'

'He was the best man.'

His mouth dropped. 'At the wedding?'

She nodded. 'He's Hamish's best friend. But it's OK.' She smiled saccharine sweet. 'He's still part of the family. Probably will be part of the family because now he's dating Celia.'

'Cousin Celia?' Owen felt the cold chill ripple through him. Was that why Bella had played so wildly with him? Because she'd wanted to show them all she didn't need them? Just wanted a hot date to throw in their faces? He'd known at the time that that was part of it and he'd enjoyed playing along. But once they'd been behind closed doors there'd been a genuine, raw passion in her—an intensity that he hadn't expected. And he'd found an answering need rising in him. A hunger that had been extreme and that hadn't been fully fed. He'd wanted more and had thought she did too.

Now he knew better. So that wildness had purely been

driven by rebound and pride? No wonder she hadn't wanted to know him after and had given him a false number. He'd just been a convenient tool for the evening. His fingers curled tighter round his cutlery. Maybe he wasn't going to bide his time after all. Maybe he would have a go for the way she'd treated him that night—right about now.

But Bella was still talking. 'They're all so pleased, because he is such a great guy,' she continued. 'But of course, they do feel for me. I mean, it must be so hard, seeing him with my cousin like that. After he broke my heart and all. But he just fell in love with Celia, you see. And she really is his perfect match.'

Owen stared at her for a second, not sure if she was being sarcastic or not. Then he caught the glint in her eye. And he started to laugh. Couldn't help it, and the knot of tension loosened again.

Bella smiled too. 'I can see the funny side. I can. But they all think he broke up with me. They just can't believe that I'd have ditched him. It's beyond their comprehension that someone like me would have thrown away a catch like him.'

It soothed him no end to hear she'd been the one to dump the jerk. 'Does what they think really matter so much?'

'Maybe it shouldn't.' She looked at her clear plate. 'But it does.'

'Why?'

'I just want them to respect me.' She pushed back her chair and stood. 'I want them to respect what I do.'

Owen stood, picked up his plate and headed after her. He could see some of the problem. It might be hard, for the conservative type her family seemed to be, to respect someone who wore a Walt Disney dress and drove a car called Bubbles.

He followed her back inside, down the stairs, struggling with the fact his desire for her wasn't abating at all. How was he going to manoeuvre this the way he wanted? Could he really do patience?

'So what was the best bit of the day?' He put his plate on the bench, near where she now stood, filling the sink with hot water and detergent. 'Assuming there was a best bit.'

She turned and smiled then, a brilliant, genuine smile that made him snatch a quick breath.

'Seeing my sister so happy.'

Bella could see she'd surprised him. She rinsed the plates and pots and stacked them in the dishwasher. She felt a bit embarrassed about all she'd just unloaded—but once she'd started babbling she couldn't stop and it meant there weren't those heavy silences. The last thing she'd wanted was to sound like some little girl whining about her family not taking her seriously. She was hard to take seriously because she did tend to make stupid mistakes. But that didn't mean that what she did contribute wasn't worthwhile.

She certainly hadn't meant to harp on about Rex. Celia could have him. She honestly didn't want him. He wasn't her type at all. And based on what she could see around she was determined to think Owen wasn't either. People who had this kind of success were conservative, weren't they? They worked hard, played safe, climbed to the top—from the looks of things Owen was definitely at the top. And conservative people just didn't 'get' Bella. No wonder he'd skipped out as soon as he could. No wonder he was Mr Reluctant now. She refused to embarrass him by throwing herself at him. She would be nice, polite, not make a fool of herself—any more than she already had. But she couldn't help appreciating his closeness as he sorted out the dishwasher and switched it on.

'I'm really tired,' she said. 'It's been quite a day.'

'Sure has,' he agreed—those soft, gentle tones again like on the beach as they'd headed to her studio.

Heart thudding, she turned, quickly, awkwardly, to head to her room. But just as she was about to leave it hit her how kind he'd been. He hadn't lectured her about her many mishaps of the day, hadn't teased her mercilessly as her family and friends would have. He'd just accepted it. Dealt with it. Helped her.

And she really appreciated it.

She turned back, still feeling completely awkward. 'Owen, thank you,' she began formally.

He walked up to her then and, now she'd looked up at him, he captured her gaze with his—with the vivid intensity of it. He put a finger on her lips and she was held fast.

'Leave it. It's not a problem.'

Like a statue she stood, mesmerised once more, filled with the memory of how well they'd fitted together. How wonderful his body had felt. How much she'd like to feel it again.

His focus dropped, flickered over her face and then lower. His finger followed, leaving her mouth to touch the hollow just below her collarbone, brushing back her blouse to reveal the skin. 'Is this new?'

What? Oh, the unicorn, the fake tattoo she always wore for parties. She put one on all the kids too. It was part of the fairy ritual.

'It's temporary,' she whispered. She didn't know why she was whispering, it was just that her voice wouldn't go any louder as his thumb smoothly stroked the small spot.

And at her words a touch of seriousness dulled the gleam in his eyes. A half-smile curved one side of his mouth, but it wasn't one of tease or wicked intent. He stepped back. 'Sleep well.'

Disappointment wafted through her. So he wasn't interested. It had been a night of craziness for him and not one he wanted to repeat. For now she was back in his life but only, like her tattoo, temporary.

What had happened today might not be a problem for him. But it was for her.

CHAPTER SEVEN

OWEN sat back in his chair, letting the debate wash over him as two of his young design team warred over the best way to progress a new program they were working on. They had a meeting with the client in just an hour's time and they had to decide before then. He watched disinterestedly as they both tried to secure his vote with impassioned speeches aimed in his direction. He wasn't really listening.

He hadn't seen Bella leave this morning. Figured she must be on an early shift at the café she was working at. The fairy dress that had haunted him all night was slung over one of the chairs so he knew she hadn't skipped out on him already. Although he suspected she wanted to. He studied the fabric, saw her in it in his mind's eye. The outfit was demure, no parents would object, and yet she looked so damn sexy, so edible. Like a silver-wrapped bon bon—one that he wanted to unpeel and devour in one big bite. No wonder she was asked if she did adult parties. He'd been awake all hours, still seeing her in it—and the curve of her breast almost *not* in it.

She had this whole slightly incompetent thing going—she had a car that looked as if it had a bad case of multicoloured measles and tyres so bald you could practically see your reflection in them. As for the hard-boiled eggs... He could still feel the mortification that had emanated from her in great waves. It hadn't been hard not to laugh. Unlike her neighbours and the firefighters, he'd seen under the blushes to the hurt beneath, and the fear. The clarity of it all surprised him. He wasn't usually one to tune into the deep feelings of others, but with her it had been so acute he'd almost felt it himself. And crazily he didn't want her to feel alone. He didn't want her to *be* alone. Alarming, when being alone was the one thing he liked best.

But she'd been faced with a situation where she'd been feeling desperate—desperate enough to come home with him, because he knew she hadn't wanted to. And that, despite those occasional signs pointing the other way, made him keep the brakes on.

She hadn't wanted to see him again—had deliberately given him the wrong number—and then had been forced to accept his assistance. Assistance he'd been careful to offer casually—knowing instinctively that if he'd come on strong she'd refuse and he hadn't wanted that. Because he was certain there was still a strong attraction there—she might not like it, but the chemical reaction between them was undeniable.

Now, somehow, he was going to find out why she didn't like it, and then he was going to get rid of it.

It slowly dawned on him that the room had descended into silence. They were all looking his way. And then he saw that the attention of his team wasn't on him or the lack of conversation. They were all fixated on a spot over his shoulder.

He heard slightly laboured breathing and turned to look behind him. And he was glad he was sitting down. Because the zip on his trousers was instantly pulled really tight. If he were to stand it would be obvious to all the world what this woman did to him. As it was he might have given it away with his mouth hanging open for the last—how long was it already?

She was standing only a few paces into the room, the door to her bedroom open behind her. She was wearing an old, thin, white tee shirt. It was oversized, the sleeves coming to her elbows, the hem only just covering the tops of her thighs. Good thing it reached even that far because that, it seemed, was it. Her only other adornment was a thin white cord coming from each ear, in her hand the tiny MP3 player. Even from this distance, in the silence of his colleagues, he could hear the faint strains of the music playing in her ears.

He clawed back the ability to move and glanced at the table, catching the surreptitious smiles between his workers and saw Billy openly staring at her. He couldn't blame him. He swung his face back towards her himself, unable to look away for long.

Her mouth had opened. She might have apologised but it wasn't audible. He saw her take in another deep shuddering breath. And then she turned, and walked back into the bedroom. As she'd moved her breasts had moved too, making it more than clear that there was no bra on under there.

'Excuse me.' Her voice was louder that time, her profile fiery as she darted back into the bedroom.

Owen stared after her. She had surprisingly long legs for someone who really wasn't that tall. He remembered them around his waist and wanted to wrap them there again—preferably *now*.

Instead he turned his head back to his team.

'One sec, guys,' he managed to mutter. He swivelled his chair right around before standing so his back was to them as he rose. Gritting his teeth and praying for self-control, he headed after her.

She was across the other side of the room, but turned back to the door as he entered. He glanced about for a moment to buy some more control time before looking at her again. The glance took in her rumpled bed. It didn't help his focus.

'I'm so sorry,' she mumbled, cheeks still stop-sign red. 'I was listening to my music and didn't hear you all out there.'

'I should have warned you, but I thought you'd gone. We have meetings up here every so often.'

All he wanted to do was slide his fingers under the hem of that ratty old shirt and find out for sure if her bottom truly was as bare as her legs were. Looking down, he could see the outline of her nipples. Her glorious, soft warm breasts that he longed to cup in his hands and kiss as he had that magical night on Waiheke.

He was twisting up inside with the effort of trying to control his want, knowing he had to get back to that meeting when all he wanted was to back her up against the bed and take her. The way he was feeling right now it wouldn't take long. Just a few minutes. Fast and furious.

But he knew it wouldn't be enough. He needed longer with her—he needed a whole night.

'I'll be on my way in a moment.' She was still mumbling.

He looked into her face then and the hunger in it jolted him. She was staring—as if she hadn't seen him before, her silvery blue eyes wide. He wondered if she knew how transparent they were. The desire shone in them, the dazed surprise as she looked him over. But at the back of them he could also see hesitation. And that was the bit he didn't understand. What had happened that night? And how could he right it? Nothing could happen until he did. He wanted her as willing and as wild as she'd been at the beginning.

So with sheer force of will he turned away, and, acting as normally as he could, went back to his incredibly boring meeting.

When she emerged from the bedroom the next time she

was clothed in the black trousers and shirt he figured was her work attire. He rose and walked her to the door, shielding her from the overly curious stares of his colleagues. He bet they'd be curious. They'd never seen a woman here before. He was glad she'd emerged from one of the spare rooms. He knew he had a reputation for short term, and that was a reputation and a reality that he wanted to keep. It was a good way of keeping gold-diggers at bay. But he wasn't glad about the way Billy was still eyeing her up.

'Are you going to the café?' Of course she was, but he wanted to have some sort of conversation with her, wanted to hold her there for just a fraction longer.

She nodded, still not looking at him, clearly eager to escape.

'But you haven't had breakfast.'

'I'll have something at work.'

She'd slipped out the door before he could think of anything else stupid to say.

He usually worked most of the day up in his apartment, liking the light and the space to think freely—away from the phones and noise of his employees. But today, after the meeting, he stayed down on the second floor with them. Keeping away from the sight of that damn dress and the scent of her.

He was going to have to win her over again. How? Make her laugh? Do something nice for her? He had the suspicion he needed to be careful about that—she'd got huffy over his offer to take care of her car. So what, then?

Annoyed with himself for spending so long thinking about her, he forced himself to work longer and harder. And when that failed he went out and got physical.

Bella had had a long day. She was well used to working in a café but was more tired than usual from standing and smiling for so many hours. She'd spent the whole time seeing Owen looking the ultimate stud in that suit. Devastating, distracting, delicious—and totally beyond her reach.

Now she was sitting at his big table, desperately trying to sew the sleeve back onto the offending fairy dress. She'd had a call from one of the parents who'd been at yesterday's party. She had a four-year-old niece who was having a party this weekend and would she be able to attend? Of course she would. She needed the money too badly to say no. She needed to get out of Owen's apartment before she threw herself at him desperate-wench style.

Sighing, she tried to thread the needle again. She was having more luck with her party entertaining than she was with her serious acting. She'd phoned up one of the theatres and had felt totally psyched out when the artistic director started asking about what training she'd had and so on. She'd stumbled, like the amateur she was. He'd said they had nothing now but to keep an eye out in the paper for the next auditions call. She didn't know what else she'd expected, but it was disheartening all the same.

Then Owen got home. She stared as he gave her a brief grin and headed to the kitchen. He'd been to the gym or for a run or something because he was in shorts and a light tee and trainers and there was bare brown skin on show. He was filmed in sweat and breathing hard. She was fascinated. Her own pulse skipped faster, forcing her to take in air quicker too.

He reached into the fridge and pulled out a bottle of water. Seeing him swigging deeply like that, Bella totally lost her stitch. She struggled once more to rethread the needle.

He wandered closer, staring just as hard back at her with an expression she couldn't define. The thread slipped again.

'Repairs not going so well?'

Major understatement. She'd scrubbed so hard at the hem to get the wine stains out and had only partially succeeded. She was gutted because it was a one-in-a-million dress and if she didn't get it sorted she wouldn't be able to work. She couldn't afford a new one and she couldn't afford to get this one fixed. She was going to have to do it herself. She squared her shoulders. Determined to do it, refusing to send an SOS to her father, refusing to give up.

'Let me have a go.' He went back to the kitchen, washed his hands, dried them and then reached for the fabric.

Stunned, she handed it over. 'You really were some sort of Boy Scout?'

He glanced at her then, his eyes full of awareness, and she kicked herself for bringing the memory of that night out into the open. She flushed.

He looked back to the needle, lips twitching. 'Actually, no, but I figure I can't do as bad a job as you are.'

'Thanks very much.'

He sat in the chair next to hers. Suddenly antsy, she moved and took a quick walk around the room before returning to stand over him. He'd been out running for over an hour. She could see the '68' minutes frozen on his stopwatch where he'd recorded his time. Yet his breathing was now normal. Fit guy. But then she knew that already. She could feel the heat from him and all it did was make her uncomfortably hot and her breath came shorter and faster still—as if she were the one out marathon training.

He didn't look too competent with the needle, though.

'Damn.'

Sure enough he'd pricked his finger.

She felt mightily glad to see he was a little useless at something.

He looked up at her, his eyes suddenly all puppy-dog apologetic. 'Sorry,' he said. 'Tell you what, I'll get my dry-cleaner to take it—they do mending as well.'

'No.' She shook her head.

'Bella, I have to. I've smeared blood on it now. I owe you.'

She looked at the dress; sure enough, there was a big spot right on the cute capped sleeve.

'Oh.' Her heart lurched.

'It's the least I can do.' He really did look sorry. 'I'm sure they'll be able to fix it.'

She hadn't got the wine stains out. She'd have no luck getting the blood mark either. Damn it, he'd put her in the position of having to accept his help again. 'OK.'

He slung the dress back over the chair. 'They'll have it back in twenty-four hours.'

Just as he turned away she caught sight of his wicked grin and the suspicion that he'd done it deliberately flew at her. She opened her mouth to protest, but the words died on her tongue as she thought about it. She loved that dress. She *needed* that dress. She could pay him back after the party, couldn't she? She really had no option.

'I'm starving.' He stretched. 'Let's do pizza.'

Take-out pizza she could handle. It was cheap; it was yummy. Her sense of independence surged. Hell, she could even buy it.

'Just give me a couple of minutes to shower and change,' he called as he headed to his room.

She was opening all the kitchen cupboards and drawers when he got back.

'Looking for something?'

'Phonebook,' she muttered.

He stared at her quizzically for a moment. 'Ever heard of the Internet? Anyway, we're not ordering in, we're going out.'

'We are?' Nonplussed, she stared at him. Since when? But he was halfway to the door already.

She called after him as he sped down the stairs. 'Going out where?'

He grinned up at her as she descended the last few hundred steps. 'My favourite.'

It was a colourful Italian restaurant about five doors down from his warehouse. Not quite the cheap and cheerful she'd imagined. More refined than relaxed, but they didn't seem to mind his casual jeans and shirt and her charity shop special skirt.

Bella had kittens as she read the menu—and saw the prices. Owen seemed to read her mind. 'My treat. A further apology.'

That was the point where she finally baulked. 'No.' She was not going to have him call all the shots like this, and certainly not have him *pay* for everything. It made the situation sticky.

'Pardon?' He looked at her. The air almost crackled.

'No, thank you,' she enunciated clearly. 'You've already done far too much for me, Owen.'

He'd frozen. Clearly he didn't hear the word no very often. She was going to have to remedy that. 'You don't have any brothers or sisters, do you?' she asked.

'No,' he said, surprised. 'How did you figure that?'

'You're too used to getting your own way.'

He stared at her; she met the scrutiny with a determined lift to her chin. 'You think?' He suddenly stood. 'Let's get out of here, then. We'll do your precious takeaway.'

'*I'm* paying.' Assertiveness plus, that was the way.

'Fine.' His lips were twitching again.

The rooftop was as warm and seductive as the night before and Bella soon realised she would have been far safer in the overpriced restaurant. Desperately she went for small talk—anything to distract her from how hot he looked, how hot she felt. And to stop her from making a fool of herself. 'Where are your parents?'

'Mum's in Auckland, Dad's in Australia.'

So they'd split up. Somehow it didn't surprise her. 'Were you very old when they busted up?'

He looked cynically amused, as if he knew how she was analysing him. 'I was nineteen.'

'Really?'

Owen smiled at her surprise. 'Twenty-three years of marriage gone. Just like that.'

'Did one of them have an affair?'

'No,' he answered. Not to his knowledge. But that was the point, wasn't it? He hadn't known about any of it. He'd been so obtuse. Maybe it would have been easier if one of them had. 'They just grew apart.'

She was frowning. 'So what, they just woke up one day and decided to call it quits?'

That was how it had seemed to him at first. A bolt from the blue. Utterly unexpected, unforeseen. But if he'd had an ounce of awareness, he would have known. It still pained him that two of the most important people in his life had been slowly imploding and he hadn't even noticed. He'd been too preoccupied with himself and his work and all his great plans.

'They were unhappy for a long time. I never knew. I was too busy with school and sport and socialising to notice. But they agreed to stick together until I was through school and then separate. In those teen years it seemed every other mate's parents were busting up. I thought mine were the shining example of success. Turns out they just wanted to protect me— stop me going off the rails like so many of those mates then did.'

He didn't want to know that level of ignorance again. Part of him was angry with them for not being honest with him sooner, part of him respected them for the way they'd loved him. More of him was angry with himself for being so blind. And he couldn't be sure that he wouldn't be that blind again, so he wasn't up for that kind of risk.

She'd stopped eating her pizza and was staring at him with such expressive eyes, it jabbed him inside to look into them. He stared at the box between them instead and kept on talking to cover it.

'I think they got bored with each other. They had different interests. The only thing holding them together was me.' Together forever just wasn't a reality—not for anyone. If his parents couldn't make it, no one could. He cleared his throat. 'It wasn't acrimonious or anything. Don't think it left me scarred or anything. We can all get together and do dinner. They were both totally supportive when I decided to quit university to concentrate on developing my company.'

Not scarred? Bella doubted that. This was the man who swore never to marry. Who said it wasn't worth the paper it was written on. While many men could claim commitment-phobia, his seemed more vehement than most. If that wasn't scarred she didn't know what was. But maybe there was more to it. Her newly assertive, independent persona took a bite of pizza and went for it.

'And so you've just been working on your company ever since? No serious girlfriend?'

'What is this?' Irritation flashed. 'The Spanish Inquisition?'

So there was someone. 'Just answer.' She pointed her pizza at him. 'Has there really been no one serious in your life?'

'All right.' He took a huge bite of pizza and answered out the side of his mouth. 'I had a girlfriend. A long time ago.' Then he shut his lips and chomped hard.

'What happened?'

He shrugged, eventually swallowed. 'Nothing much.'

'Did you live together?' Why did she need all the details? She couldn't help but want all the details.

'For a while.'

The niggle of jealousy was bigger than she expected. 'What happened?'

'She met someone else. They're married now. Has a kid— two maybe.'

She stared at him, shocked. 'She *left* you?'

He looked levelly at her. 'I'm not a good companion, Bella.'

'What makes you say that?' Good grief, the guy was gorgeous.

'When I'm working on a project, that's my world, that's all there is. For those weeks, months, whatever, other things pass me by.'

She frowned. 'Are you working on something now?'

'Yes.'

Yet it seemed to her that nothing much passed him by. 'You don't think you're being a little hard on yourself?'

'I didn't notice my folks falling apart. I didn't notice her falling apart.' His face hardened. 'I'm selfish, Bella, remember?'

She stared, her mental picture elsewhere, thinking. From what she'd seen of him, it didn't quite ring true—yes, he did what he wanted, but he did what others wanted too. But he'd totally closed over now, moodily staring at the half-eaten pizza.

She wanted to lighten the mood. 'So what, you just lock yourself away and do geeky boy hacker things?'

His blue eyes met hers and sparked again. 'I have program-mers who build the software, Bella. Then I use the programs to do the work that needs doing.'

'I'm surprised you need the programmers, Owen,' she

teased, pleased to have his humour back. 'Why don't you get all your precious computers to do it all for you?'

He chuckled. 'There's one thing that computers can't do. Something that I can do really, really well.'

'What's that?'

'Imagine,' he answered softly. 'I have a really, *really* good imagination, Bella.'

She stared at him, reading everything she wanted to read in his expression—heat. She was a dreamer—her father had told her off for it. That she wouldn't get anywhere sitting in a daydream all day...

'Someone has to dream it up.'

Someone like him. He was so enticing. Did he know what she was imagining right now? She suspected he might because that look in his eye was back.

Confusion made her run for deflection. 'I could never sit at a computer all day.'

'I could never stand on my feet slaving after people all day in a ton of noise.'

'I like the noise of the café. I like watching the customers as they sit and people-watch. I like the face-to-face contact.'

'I like face to facc.'

'Really?' She didn't quite believe him. She had the feeling he holed himself away in that big apartment and thought up things her brain wasn't even capable of comprehending. And then he sold them. She'd been wrong—he was more entrepreneur than anything.

His grin turned wicked. 'And body to body.' He leaned closer, his voice lower, his eyes more intense. 'Skin to skin.'

Owen grinned as he saw the change in her eyes again. The sparkle went sultry. When he stepped close to her, when he spoke low to her, she coloured, flustered. But he wanted her more than flustered, he wanted her hot—and wild. And now he saw the way to that was so much simpler than he'd thought. All he had to do was get close to her. And she wanted to know about him? He'd tell her about him.

'A couple of years ago I sold the business to a conglomerate for many millions of dollars.' He was upfront, knowing money wasn't something that rang her bell. She seemed to take a strange joy in being broke; it was almost as if she deliberately mucked up—as if it was some sort of 'screw you' signal to her dad.

'So what did you do with all your millions?' she asked, her tone utterly astringent.

There, see? He'd known it would go down like the proverbial lead balloon. 'What do you think I did with it?'

'Bought yourself a Ferrari,' she snapped, 'and a few other boy toys. A plush pad in the centre of the city. An easy, playboy lifestyle.' Her eyes were like poisoned arrows pointing straight at him.

He batted them away. 'Yes to the Ferrari—it was my one big indulgence. But not so many other toys. As you've already seen the plush pad in the city isn't so plush—half of it still has to be plushed up.'

He paused, took in her focused attention. Good, it was time his little fairy saw things the way they actually were.

'I put half into a charitable trust and built a think tank with the other. The people you saw in that meeting yesterday have some of the brightest and best minds you'll find anywhere. Total computer geeks.' He winked at her. 'I get them together and they work through problems, building new programs.'

'That you can sell and make lots of money with.'

'That's right. We take the money, give half away and get

on with the next idea. I like ideas, Bella. I like to think them up and get them working and then I like to move on to the next big one.'

'You don't want to see them all the way through?'

He frowned. 'I don't like to get bored.' He didn't like to be complacent. He didn't like to be around long enough to 'miss' anything. It was better for him to keep his mind moving. 'As for the easy, playboy lifestyle—sure, occasionally. But for the most part I work very long, very hard.'

'Why? When you're wealthy enough to retire tomorrow?'

'Because I like it.' Because he couldn't not. Because he needed something to occupy his mind and his time. Because he was driven. Because he couldn't face the void inside him that he knew couldn't be filled. Because he was missing something that everyone else had—the compassion, the consideration, the plain awareness and empathy towards others. His relationship with Liz had made him feel claustrophobic. The family she'd threatened him with had proved to him he wasn't built for it and he had bitterly resented her for trying to force him into it. He would not allow that pressure to be put on him again. But he'd have a woman the way he wanted—he'd have Bella the way he wanted.

'For all that *success*—' he underlined the word, knowing the concept annoyed her '—I'm still the guy who made you laugh that night.' He tossed the pizza crust into the box and stood. 'I'm still the guy who made your legs so weak you couldn't stand.' He took a step back, determined to walk away now. He spoke softer. 'I'm still the guy who made you alternately sigh then scream with pleasure.' He paused. He'd leave her knowing exactly what his intentions were—plain and simple. He spoke softer still. 'And I'm the guy who's going to do it all again.'

CHAPTER EIGHT

BELLA stayed in her room until well after nine the next morning, sure that by then Owen would be downstairs overseeing his group of geeks, coming up with some program to bring about world peace or something. Last night had been the most frustrating night of her life—even more frustrating than after he'd left her bed on Waiheke, and she hadn't thought *anything* could top that.

After his outrageous comments, he'd gone. With a smile that had promised everything and threatened nothing he'd walked downstairs—presumably to his room. The door had been closed when she'd summoned the courage to leave the roof. What had she been supposed to do—follow him?

She'd badly, *badly* wanted to. But she didn't, of course, because her legs had lost all strength again—just with his words.

Now, as she moved quietly across the warehouse, she saw his bedroom door was closed. She knocked gently, just to be certain. When there was no reply she opened it and walked on in. Halfway to the bathroom door on the other side she realised that the big lump of bedding on the edge of his bed was moving; it actually had a lump in it—him. He sat up— all brown chest on white sheets, hair sticking up in all directions and wide sleepy grin. 'Good morning.'

She froze, halfway across the floor. 'I thought you'd be at work already.'

'No.' He yawned. 'I didn't get much sleep last night.'

She felt the colour flood into her face.

'I had a call from New York that went on for a while.'

Her colour continued to heighten. She started to back out of the room. At least she was wearing trackies now under the tee shirt. After the embarrassment of yesterday she wasn't running the risk of encountering all those people when she was half starkers again.

'No, don't worry,' he said, swinging his legs out of the bed and reaching for a shirt on the floor. 'Use the bathroom. I'm going for a run.'

She stopped in the doorway. He'd stood up from the bed. Naked except for the shirt he was holding to his lower belly. He was magnificent. Rippling muscles and indents and abs you wouldn't see anywhere other than the Olympic arena. He yawned again, stretched his free arm, showing his body off to complete perfection.

He was doing it deliberately. He had to be. She swallowed—once. Took a breath. Blinked. Swallowed again. Still couldn't seem to move her legs.

'Bella?'

She turned and walked then, straight back to her bedroom. Where she threw herself down and buried her burning face in the cool of the sheets.

Damn it, Owen. If you're going to do it, *do* it.

Half an hour later she figured he'd gone and be out for another hour at least. So she headed to the kitchen—she needed a long, very cold drink. As she downed the icy water she heard the door slam.

She turned, and there he was wearing loose shorts and a light tee. He was puffing, sweating a little. He stalked towards her. Straight towards her and he didn't seem to be stopping.

'You're back already,' she blurted.

'Yeah,' he muttered. To her acute disappointment he veered off course, halting and reaching into the fridge. 'It was short but intense.'

She held onto her glass, leaned back against the sink and stared.

'I ran up and down the stairs for twenty minutes.'

She quickly lowered her glass to the bench. He stood facing her, strong and fit, and she was breathing harder than he. It was early morning, broad daylight, she was stone-cold sober, and she wanted him more than she'd ever wanted anything.

He leaned back, resting on the bench opposite her. 'What are you thinking?'

'N-nothing.'

There was a silence where he looked at her with such amused disbelief and she wanted to squirm away from the knowledge in his eyes.

'Come here.'

She hesitated.

'Here.'

She walked, one whole step, aiming for nonchalant, before stopping, stupidly wishing she weren't still wearing her loose, ugly trackies and old tee shirt.

'Come right here.'

'What?' she asked as she moved fractionally closer, her mind tickled with an alternative meaning to his words, and a delicious mix of anticipation and alarm rose when he straightened. She took another tiny step.

'Why don't you do the "nothing" you've been thinking

about for the last five minutes?' He smiled then, took a step to meet her when she stopped short. 'Or is it longer that you've been thinking about "nothing"?'

Her mouth opened but nothing came out.

His gaze dropped to it; she could almost feel him roving over the curves and contours of her lips. She desperately wanted him to. His eyes flicked, coming back to snare hers. There was that warmth in them, the glow was back—the light that had seduced her so completely on Waiheke. And she couldn't walk away from it.

She knew he was waiting. But she was frozen. And then it seemed that words might not be necessary.

His breathing was more rapid now too—faster than when he'd first got back from his run. And the glow in his gaze had become a burn that was steadily gaining in intensity.

A shrill, tuneless series of beeps shattered the silence.

He didn't step away. 'Someone's trying to call you.'

She shook her head, unable to tear her gaze from his. 'It's just my phone telling me it's almost out of battery.'

'Recharge it.'

'I can't,' she confessed. 'I left the power cord at my flat.'

A smile stole into his eyes. The phone whistled the ugly tune again.

He reached forward, slipping his hand into her pocket and pulling out the phone. She thought, hoped, he was going to throw it away. But then he looked away from her, flipped it open and stared at it. Frowned. Pushed a couple of buttons.

'What's wrong? Is it not working?'

His head jerked in negation. 'I have a cord that should work with this,' he muttered, but his mind had clearly moved to something else. Suddenly she wanted her phone back. She reached, but he held it up high, still pressing buttons.

'What are you looking for?' she asked.

'Tony's Lawn Mowing Service.'

'What?'

'That was the number you gave me.' He gave her a hard look. 'That was why I couldn't get through to you. The phone number you gave me was completely wrong.'

Oh. Hell. 'Was it?' Her voice sounded weak, even to her.

He shot an even harder look. 'Accidentally on purpose.'

Her face fired up. The tension between them burst through her defences. 'You were in such a hurry to leave. I didn't want to be sitting around half hoping for you to call. Better to knock it out there and then.'

He moved, tossing the phone to the side, taking the last step forward so he was smack in front of her, blocking her exit. 'Only *half* hoping?' His smile teased but his eyes were laser sharp.

Her blush deepened and inside she wanted to beat her head against a wall—so he *had* tried. Now she felt more defensive than ever. 'Well, you didn't bother to give me your number,' she said miserably. 'Or even tell the truth about where you were staying.'

'That was irrelevant. At the time I was focused on making sure I could contact you. I knew there was no point giving you my number. You never would have called me. Would you?'

Her blush deepened. No. She never would. She'd been too mortified at the way he'd slunk off into the night. 'You just up and left me.' Even she heard it—how much her words betrayed her.

His smile twitched. 'I can see I have some work to do.'

'What sort of work?'

'Convincing you how much I want you. How much I wanted to stay that night.'

'If you'd wanted to stay, you could have.' A little petulant, still unforgiving.

He shook his head. 'Responsibilities, Bella. People were relying on me.'

'Priorities. Choices.' She'd been relying on him. Unfair of her perhaps, but she'd fallen—just like that. And she'd wanted him by her side. She'd enjoyed having him as a buffer between her and her family. But even more, she'd just wanted him at her side again—*in*side.

'I had every intention of calling you. I tried to call you.' He paused. 'You were the one who made the choice to stop that from happening.'

Humiliation at her exposure rose. Yes, she'd deliberately sabotaged any chance he might make contact because she'd been so sure he wouldn't and she didn't want to keep on hoping for ever that he would. Because she would have hoped—hoped and hoped and gone on hoping for evermore. And at the same time she'd been so sure he wouldn't. She didn't want to be that much of a loser any more.

His fingers were gentle but quite firm on her jaw as he turned her face back to him. He spoke very clearly. 'What you have yet to learn, Bella, is that I let very little stand in the way of what I want.'

'And what do you want?'

'You.'

She was melting inside, every bone liquefying.

'And the thing is…' he inched closer '…I get the distinct impression that you want me too.'

She was about to puddle at his feet. 'Owen—'

'Now why don't you do what you've been thinking about? Because that's exactly what I'm going to do.'

Her breathing skittered as he stepped closer again.

'I'm going to touch you and kiss you and feel you and watch you.'

She'd forgotten to blink and her eyes felt huge and dry.

'I want to watch you, Bella.' He was so close now. If she moved less than a millimetre, she'd be touching him.

'Do you know how expressive you are? How wide your eyes go when you want something? How pink your cheeks and your lips go?' His voice dropped as he whispered in her ear. 'How wet you get?'

She sucked in a breath. Shaken and very, very stirred. Did he know how wet she was now?

'Do it, Bella,' he urged in that low, sexy whisper. 'Do it.'

Her hand lifted and she spoke without thinking. A whisper, softer than his. 'Take your shirt off.'

For a moment their eyes met and she trembled at the flare of passion in the blue of his.

His hands moved to his top and with a fast movement he whipped it off, tossing it in a direction similar to her phone. He glanced down. The sweat had tracked down, slightly matting the fine layer of hair.

'I should shower.' The first hint of self-consciousness she'd ever seen in him.

'Not yet.' She placed the hand she'd raised on his chest, spreading her fingers on the heat, liking the dampness. She leant forward, licking the hollow at the base of his throat, tasting the salt. She liked him like this—raw, his body already primed for action. The run had just been the warm-up.

His breath hissed out.

Glancing down, she saw just how much he did want this— how much he wanted her. She looked back up and saw he'd seen her checking him out, and his smile had gone sinful.

His hands slipped down, pushing the old tracksuit pants

from her waist and down. She kicked them off as he unclasped her bra, then he pulled each strap down her arms so it fell from her. Underneath the tee shirt her breasts were now free.

'Tell me, the other day when you barged in on my meeting wearing this gorgeous old tee shirt, were you wearing panties beneath it?'

Bella hesitated. A smile slowly curving her mouth. 'What do you think?'

His smile grew too. 'I'm thinking no.'

'I think you might be right.'

'We'd better get them off, then.'

He dropped to his haunches, slipped his fingers to her hips and found the elastic of her undies. He tugged and she wiggled—just a fraction—so they slid down. As she stepped out of them she stepped closer to him. He stayed down, looking back up at her.

'Perfect.'

His fingers moved slowly over her thighs, his broad palms warm and smooth as they stroked.

He stood. 'I've been dreaming of you in this shirt ever since ten twenty-five yesterday morning.' Then he kissed her—his mouth moving over hers, his tongue invading with hungry surges, until she was breathless and giddy and he groaned.

'I am having that shower,' he said, taking her hand and leading her to his bedroom. 'Stay there, I'll be two minutes.' He kissed her again. 'Make that one.'

But now that Bella had taken the step, she wasn't letting him get away. She followed him into the bathroom, laughing as he grabbed the shower gel. Sobering as she watched him lather it in his hands, slap it onto his body, and seeing again how truly magnificent he was.

'Bella, if you keep looking at me like that I—'

'I haven't showered either.' She cut him off. Tee shirt and all, she followed him into the steam.

The water ran over her, making the cotton of the tee shirt thick and heavy. It clung to her. He cupped her breast through the sodden fabric, thumb stroking the taut nipple. She rubbed the soapy bubbles over his skin, starting with his shoulders, his chest and then lower.

'Bella…' There was definite warning in his tone. And then he growled, yanked her into his arms and kissed her hard, his hands keeping her close.

The elation ran through her as she tasted his desire, thrilled with the knowledge that it matched her own.

He kissed her until her knees went weak and standing was becoming a major issue. She clung to his shoulders, not wanting to break the bliss of the kiss.

Slowly he peeled the wet tee shirt up and off her body. It landed on the bathroom floor with a loud smack. He flipped the lever and shut off the water. The sudden silence was broken by the occasional drip. But the steam kept rising.

He took a step towards her, and with an impish smile, she took a step back. His eyes lit up so she took another, and another, and then with a giggle she turned and ran, exhilarated as she sensed his speed behind her. It was only a second or two and he'd caught her, dragging them both the last half-metre to the bed, and there they tumbled and rolled.

He rose above her, on all fours, trapping her between his legs, her hands in his. For a moment they paused, both enthralled and excited by the chase—and her surrender.

She deliberately relaxed, parted her legs, and sent him the invitation. He didn't need it. He was already taking—mastering her body by using the magic of his. His hands caressed, his lips kissed and his eyes promised. And within moments she was arching, her hips up high, the tension ready to burst. He kissed her again, so intimately, his mouth fastening onto her clitoris while his fingers played deep within.

Her hands clenched in the thickness of his hair as, oh, so quickly she was there, on the brink and over, her body shaking, twisting beneath his.

'Again,' he demanded, slipping up her body fast, his hand still between her legs. '*Again.*' He kissed her hard while his fingers were unrelenting. Slipping and sliding and teasing as he kissed her she felt the sensation inside bridge. His tongue thrust into her mouth and she shook with the need to have that other part of him deep inside her, plunging hard and fast—stirring her to an even greater ecstasy.

She broke free of his kiss as the breath expelled harshly from her lungs and her hips bucked. 'Yes!' she cried, incredulous as one orgasm moved into another, longer, more intense one. And he watched, a fiendishly satisfied grin lighting him as she shuddered beneath him.

And then, instead of that weightless, warm, replete feeling that usually came after ecstasy, she was filled with a ravenous void, the need for completion. It was an overpowering hunger. An intense ache that angered her and drove her to take in a way she'd never done before.

She spoke to him. Short, harsh words while her hands reached out, greedily touching him, and then her mouth too. And the look of smug arrogance and amusement left his features. Concentration took over, and suddenly he was as exposed as she, his hunger revealed as her words stripped him of his control.

She watched as his breathing became laboured, revelled in his haste to sheath himself with the condom. He swore when it took too long. Swore louder when she took over and teased it down on him cruelly slow, all the while whispering in a way that was clearly driving him to distraction, pausing now and then to press passionate, open kisses across his chest. Her hands worked over his body, pulling him to her. She wriggled beneath him, rocking against him, rotating, telling him not just with her words but with her body how hot she was for him. How badly she wanted him and was wanting him more with every passing moment.

'Now, now, now!' she cried, desperate for the fullness that only he could give. And with a raw growl he responded, thrusting deep.

'Har— Oh, yes! Like that. Like that.' She didn't need to say it. He was already doing it exactly how she wanted. Hard and fast, surging into her, and she worked to meet him, stroke for stroke, her fingers curling into his strong hips.

She was transported into a magical realm where her wickedest, wildest fantasy became raw reality and much, much better—and she told him. What he was doing to her, how he was doing it so incredibly and how much more she wanted.

Until the words would no longer come because her mind could no longer think and it was squeals and sighs and moans that escaped—she couldn't control anything any more. Her hunger, her desire, her response to the pleasure his body brought her. The tension mounted—nothing before had ever been so extreme as this. Until it snapped and spasms ravaged through her, the sensations heightened by his fierce growl and the power he plunged into her.

He rolled to the side, pulling her over so her head rested on his rapidly rising chest. He chuckled then. A warm, contented sound. 'I have never been so turned on in all my life as when you were beneath me begging like that.'

Embarrassment curled into her. She'd behaved like some
sex-starved animal. She'd used words she never *thought,* let
alone voiced. Bella instantly felt the need to retain even some
sense of the upper hand. 'I wasn't begging.'

'No?'

'I was ordering,' she declared. 'Demanding, in fact.'

He yanked gently on her hair, tipping her face up so she
could see his smile.

'Do it any time. I don't mind.' It was a light, teasing smile.
'I didn't think sex could get better than that night on Waiheke.
Now I know different. That was fantastic.' He kissed her then.
A slow, sweet kiss. One kiss turned into another. When his
hand brushed between her thighs, she flinched.

He broke the kiss immediately, a concerned look in his
eyes. 'You OK?'

'Just a bit sensitive.' She flushed. So much pleasure had
brought her body to the point of pain.

He kissed her again. Gentle, relaxing kisses that soothed
the intense over-sensitivity in her body—changing it to
warm softness.

'We'll go slow this time.'

Bella had the feeling it was too late to be going slow at
anything.

CHAPTER NINE

'I HAVE to get to the café.' Bella was on another late shift today. 'Shouldn't you be in a meeting or something?'

'Or something,' Owen muttered drowsily.

Bella moved, trying to slide from the bed, but his big heavy arm tightened, penning her in. 'I have to go,' she protested weakly. 'I can't be late.'

He groaned. But his arm relaxed.

She showered quickly, dressed. He was asleep when she went to leave. She spent a second or two by the bed, simply appreciating his tousled sexiness—even in sleep he was all consuming, all powerful—taking up most of the mattress.

And the flame of delight—of disbelief—glowed brighter in her heart. He'd tried to call her. He still wanted her. Relief, joy, satisfaction—she couldn't wipe the smile from her face. For once it seemed she was going to get something she really wanted. Maybe Lady Luck had finally turned her way.

She was halfway through her shift when she checked her mobile. It had been ominously quiet—despite Owen recharging it for her. Of course it was quiet—she'd accidentally switched it off. She put it back on and cleared the messages. There were three from her landlord. She listened, wincing at his increasingly irate tones, then drew breath and dialled his number.

Less than three minutes later he was no longer her land-lord. Her lease was terminated with immediate effect. He was keeping her deposit as payment for the door and incon-venience. She had the next day to remove the rest of her be-longings.

In her break she went to the nearest ATM and got an account balance. She didn't really need to—she already knew the situation was dire. She had to save everything for a couple of weeks to get the bond for a new place. That meant she either had to stay with Owen or hit her family for another loan.

She knew what she wanted to do. But was it wise? Two weeks was a little longer than two days. They hadn't talked about anything remotely heavy like what, if any, future they had. She didn't want to—she already knew. Owen had told her right from the start that he didn't do commitment.

She'd swallow her pride and ask her father. It was in-evitable anyway; she was as incompetent as he'd always said. Couldn't even manage a month on her own without stuffing up somehow and needing help.

When she got home later in the evening, Owen was waiting for her, music playing on the seriously fancy stereo, dinner keeping warm in the oven.

'What's up?' he asked the instant he saw her.

Was she that transparent?

'I've been turfed out of the flat. The landlord is keeping my bond. I'm going to—'

'Don't worry about it,' he interrupted carelessly, putting plates on the tray. 'You can stay here, long as you need to.'

Her spirits lifted and sank in the one moment. She hadn't wanted to call on her father, but she didn't particularly want to be in Owen's debt either—no more than she already was. Besides, he didn't do live-in lovers.

'Heaven forbid.'

He turned a startled gaze on her. 'What do you mean "heaven forbid"?'

She grinned, hoping to come across light but inside kind of terrified about his response. 'That's what you said at the bar on Waiheke when I asked if you had a live-in lover.'

He lifted a large iron casserole dish out of the oven, using a couple of tea towels to cover his hands. He carefully placed it on a protective mat on the bench. Only then did he answer—equally light in tone. 'Bella, we were in a bar flirting and being flippant.'

He began ladling the steaming contents of the dish onto their plates. 'I never knew you remembered everything I said so perfectly.'

Everything he'd ever said she'd committed to memory. If only she could learn her lines with the same skill.

'Anyway, you're only staying here till you sort out a new place of your own, right?' *Not* as his live-in lover, but a temporary guest. He was making the point subtly, but nonetheless still making it. Fair enough.

'Absolutely,' she agreed. They were just confirming everything—mainly because she felt the need for well-defined boundaries.

'So,' he added, 'we don't need the labels, right? You're a friend staying here.'

'Sleeping with you.' There was that small point.

'Till you've got your new place sorted,' he continued, ignoring her comment, starting to sort eating utensils.

'Is that when we stop sleeping together?' She held her breath.

He stopped fussing in the cutlery drawer and looked at her. 'We stop sleeping together when one or other of us says the word.' He fished out another fork, put it by the plates and caught her eyes with his own once more—not that it was hard; she couldn't seem to stop staring at him. 'And says the word *gently,* right?'

Right.

He left the tray and put his hands around her waist instead. 'Rules established?' he asked softly.

'I think so.' Better late than never, she figured.

Bed buddies. An indefinite series of one-night stands. Except if she thought about it she'd wonder whether this might be more to her than a one-night stand. She might not be that old or that experienced, but even she could see this could lead to trouble—for her at any rate. So she vowed to keep that limit on it—two weeks. She'd have as much of him as she wanted—and she really wanted—then she'd move out and end it all. Before her heart as well as her body got entwined.

Early the next morning she went to the flat and cleared out the last of her belongings. Gave the whole place a final clean, but even so the burnt-egg smell lingered. Back at Owen's warehouse she ran a bath, sank into it for the best part of an hour and appreciated the beauty of the room. The dark colour scheme could be austere, but it wasn't. The flashes of red here and there hinted at a touch of passion—the fire she knew burned inside him. He was full of vitality, ambition, discipline, drive. The bathroom designer had got a good handle on him. It was very, very masculine. It screamed bachelor—for life. And yet, there were twin hand-basins, side-by-side mirrors— one for him and one for the lady currently in his life, huh? The overnight guest.

All his toiletries were in the drawer beneath the basin, leaving the bench space clear and uncluttered. Minimalist.

With a spurt of defiance she lined up her bubble bath, shower gel, shampoo and assorted moisturisers in pump bottles. So she wasn't his live-in lover? She was just a friend staying? Fine, but she was quite determined to make her mark.

He was working at the computer when she got home from the café late in the evening.

'You'll get square eyes,' she teased.

'You're not even into the Internet?' He spun on the chair to face her. 'What about the social pages?'

'I have no interest in communicating with the people I went to school with when I was five.' Not when they'd all be wealthy lawyers or doctors or married to some famous person, or anything like that, when she was just a waitress.

'But it's a necessity in today's market. You need computer skills to work.'

'I'm not saying I don't have skills. I can point and click as well as anyone, I'm just not interested. Why would I want to stare at a screen all day?'

'What about online shopping?'

'I'd really rather go to the movies.'

'And that's not staring at a screen?' He looked sardonic.

'OK, show me, then,' she challenged. 'One thing that's really interesting.'

He grinned. 'Did you know your sister has put photos of the wedding up on her chat page?'

'No.' Bella froze. 'Has she?'

'There's a really cute one of you with the stripe.'

'No!' she shrieked.

'Yep, up there for anyone and everyone to see.' He spun back to the computer, clicked a few times.

The picture was huge on the big screen. Her skin crawled

with embarrassment at the line-up of tall blonde brides-maids…and her.

'We were supposed to look like daffodils,' she said. 'Only, there's me, the lemon on the end.'

'I'd rather have a lemon any day. So much more flavour.'

She was too aghast at the pictures to feel flattered. 'Anyone can see these? *Anyone?*'

He nodded. 'I really liked this one myself.'

Another picture flashed up onto the screen. She was in the background, behind Vita and Hamish. He pressed a couple of buttons and zoomed in on her. The wind had blown the fabric tight against her chest and in the cool breeze she had the biggest case of erect nipples ever seen—you could see the outline of everything.

She felt heat rise into her cheeks, then actually felt the hardness in her nipples as he looked away from the screen, back to her, desire in his eyes.

Embarrassed, she let sarcasm mask it. 'You really are into computer porn.'

He laughed. 'Search my hard drive. There's nothing there. But I'll admit to studying this one closely for some time. It was all I had until I found out where you were.'

'Where I was?' She frowned.

'You might not have much of a presence on the web, but your sister certainly does and she gives regular updates on her and her family's activities.'

Bella was appalled. 'She's supposed to be on honeymoon. She's not supposed to be sticking things up on…' She broke off, thinking about what he'd implied. 'You *knew* I was in Wellington?'

He nodded. 'She mentions in her blog how she missed your family farewell dinner.'

'So you were in the supermarket on purpose?' Oh, my, that was sneaky.

'No,' he laughed. 'That was the Fates being kind.'

'But you knew I'd moved down here.'

He nodded.

'Were you going to keep looking for me?' Her silly heart was skipping like crazy.

'I was thinking about it.' Casually he clicked the picture away. 'Why?'

'Why do you think?' He stood, walked away from the computer and towards her. 'I told you, Bella. I tend to get what I want.'

'But you were so frosty.'

'You'd blown me off, remember? With Tony's Lawn Mowing Service.'

'Only because *you* blew *me* off,' she defended, 'and I didn't know it was Tony or anyone.' And without hesitation she went into his arms. 'Do you always *know* what you want?'

'Generally.' He didn't have to think about the answer long. 'Do you?'

Rarely. She knew what she *didn't* want, but she didn't necessarily want the opposite of that. And for once, right now, she knew exactly what she wanted.

As his arms tightened she knew what he wanted too.

'I haven't forgiven you for leaving that night,' she confessed.

'I know you haven't.'

'But do you know why?'

'You didn't want to be alone at the wedding.'

'No,' she whispered, able to admit now that that wasn't it at all. 'There were things I had planned for you.'

'Yes,' his matching whisper mocked. 'We still have unfinished business, don't we?' His hands teased. 'Now wouldn't it have been so much easier for me to find you if you had a website? I could have typed in your name and discovered you're a sexy children's party fairy—booked up all your weekends.'

She rolled her eyes. The fairy thing wasn't something she was that proud of. She didn't want all those old school friends knowing that was all her ambition had amounted to.

'I'm going to build you one,' he murmured just before pressing a kiss to her neck.

'Hmm?' Fast losing track of the conversation as his mouth took a path downwards.

'A website. For your party business. It'll take a couple of hours max.'

She stopped tufting his hair with her fingers. 'Owen, you've already done enough for me.'

'Bella, please, let me indulge my geek side.' He chuckled, his breath warming her skin. 'More to the point, let me indulge my trainee's geek side.'

But at that she chilled completely. 'You can't get your employees to build me a website.'

He lifted his head and looked unconcerned. 'Why not?'

'I can't afford to pay you.' She couldn't take more *things* from him.

He placed his forehead on hers, literally closely watching her. 'It would be a good practice job for the student placement kid. I need something to occupy his time when the team is busy on strategic stuff.'

Owen really enjoyed the challenge of getting her to agree to his help. She was always so determined to say no and he liked nothing more than hearing 'yes' from her—although more often than not it was a soft 'OK'. Pricking his finger and staining the fairy dress had been a masterstroke in solving that problem. Building her a website was more of a difficult one. He could see the argument in her eyes. But it was really no biggie and it might be a bit of a confidence boost—make her see herself as the small businesswoman she was. If she took herself seriously, others might too.

'You'd be doing me a favour.' He knew she didn't really believe him. She knew, as well as he, it was a weak argument. But Owen liked to win, it didn't matter how minor the game— and this was minor, wasn't it? Maybe not, because he decided the end justified the means in this case. So he used his best weapon. And as he kissed her the hint of her refusal drowned beneath the rising desire.

The week slipped by. He refused to let her cook—saying he knew what she did to eggs and he wasn't letting her do that kind of damage to anything else. Instead he cooked, enjoying the creativity. He never normally bothered. But night after night he had it ready for when she got home. They ate and then snuggled on the sofa while she gave him a crash course in the great movie classics, starting with *Casablanca*. He hadn't spent so much time quietly relaxing in ages. And then, through the night, they hardly relaxed at all. Voracious—the more he had, the more he wanted. The passion ran unabated and it only seemed to get better every time.

The question of her staying with him had caused a fleeting awkwardness, but he thought he'd got through it smoothly. This was still a purely temporary situation, right? But he'd suffered a sharp twinge when she'd asked about them stopping sleeping together—he definitely wasn't ready for that yet. A few more days—several more nights. It wasn't done between them.

When he went for his run one morning she went with

him—riding his bike. She didn't talk too much. Just a word here and there, and he found it companionable. When he walked into the bathroom after, the scent of her shampoo hung in the steam and disappointment surged when he saw she'd finished already. By the time he got out she was dressed and heading to the door.

'What's the hurry? I thought you were on late shift again.'

'I have an audition.' Her hair hung in a wet rope down her back.

He looked her over. 'You want me to iron that shirt for you?'

'Do you iron, Owen?'

'Not usually.' He ignored her chill. 'I have a service. But I can do it for you if you want.'

Her cool look grew even frostier. 'The only thing I iron is my hair.'

Right, yet she hadn't even bothered with that.

'It wouldn't take a second.' It was a lovely shirt, but the crease down one side didn't exactly give her the professional look.

'I'm running late as it is.'

It was his turn to frown. It was her second audition of the week—and she'd been late to that one too, had said it had gone badly, that she'd fluffed the lines completely.

But she looked so on edge now he stepped aside, letting her go.

Friday night she was on another late shift. Only he didn't feel like staying home and cooking. For once the apartment felt too big, too quiet, too lonely. He raided the fridge, found some not-too-ancient leftovers—enough to satisfy the hunger of his stomach for a while. Then he left—needing to satisfy his other hunger.

She was behind the counter, the one taking the orders, not actually making the coffee. He walked straight up to her, registering with pleasure the surprise in her eyes, the pink in her cheeks, her widening smile. The rush of warmth inside rose so fast it threw him, made him awkward. It wasn't the heat of lust; while that simmered in the background, this was different. This was a buzz, a thrill of delight caused by something else—affection, maybe? Amusement? He couldn't think what else. He took a step back, sat at the long counter facing the window so he wasn't staring straight at her. He pretended to leaf through one of the glossy magazines in the stack, but all the while he was attuned to her sing-song voice as she served the customers.

'Would you like whipped cream with that?' The teasing question had him irresistibly turning to look at her.

She was smiling—it turned sinful as she glanced at him—and everything inside suffered an electrical jolt. She could tempt a hunger striker to a four-course banquet if she asked like that. *He'd* say yes to her like a shot. His discomfort level increased when he realised it—he already *was* saying yes to her, all the damn time.

Back at Owen's house, after her shift, Bella thought how her sense of their boundaries was becoming blurry. One day he was spelling out the terms of their relationship as if it were some business transaction, the next he was incredibly sweet and telling her about his geek-boy attempt to track her down. She couldn't help but wonder if the magnetism between them was made of something stronger than just a few nights of fun.

And he was so good at getting her to agree to everything, she wanted to wrest back some of the power. Wanted to gain that independence she'd been seeking for so long. But more than that, she wanted him to be as sunk in her as she was in him—because she'd fallen for him completely now. He was beautiful, bright and bold and she wanted to keep him.

She didn't have a hope. She wasn't the sort of woman for him—if he ever wanted to commit it would be to someone super successful, beautiful, articulate. Someone who could stand beside him in any situation and do him proud. Someone like Vita. Whereas Bella would be an embarrassment—she'd be the one inadvertently wearing half her dinner on her shirt at a posh restaurant; she'd be the one falling on her face down a flight of stairs at a charity ball. She was always the one making the stupid slip-ups somehow.

But she *could* be the best sex of his life. She smothered the chuckle at the lack of loftiness in her ambition. Oh, yes, for whatever reason he wanted her body, and maybe, if she could keep him wanting her, she could keep this affair burning for longer. She wanted longer. All she had to do was trap him in some kind of sensual net—where *he* couldn't say no, where *he* couldn't get enough.

Now, in his bed, she slowly crawled down his body, towards his legs. The view he'd be getting was one she'd never be brave enough to give anyone else. But with Owen, it was different. He made no secret of how much he liked to look at her. How much just looking at her turned him on. And she wanted to turn him on really, really hard because that was what he did to her. He'd been right the other day—she had been begging—and she was determined to make him suffer to the same degree. To make him want her so much he'd never be the one to utter the words that would end it. He made her feel capable of anything—of making her most secret fantasies a reality.

Dangerous—because right now *he* was her secret fantasy.

He muttered something unintelligible. His hands came up,

moulded round the contours of her bottom, then a finger traversed through her slick heat.

'You want me to stop?' she gasped.

'Oh, no. Please, no.'

She wriggled her hips pointedly and to her mixed relief and regret his hands slipped away. At least now she could try to focus.

'Come on,' he urged. 'You're killing me.'

She nuzzled into him, her hair teasing and twisting round his erection.

'Bella…'

'Roar.'

'Tigress.' His laugh sounded half strangled.

She turned around, so she was facing him as she straddled his legs, bending so her breasts were either side of his penis. 'Watch.'

'Oh, I am.'

She took him into her mouth and twirled her tongue on the tip of him.

His hands were fisted by his sides. Every muscle in his body tensed. 'Bella, stop. Please. I want you. I want all of you.'

'I don't mind…'

He shook his head. 'I want to be inside you.'

She slid the condom down slowly.

'Bella.' His lips barely moved, jaw locked, teeth clenched.

She slid herself down even slower.

His head fell back on the bed and the sound of his groan almost made her come. She bit her lip, the tiny pain keeping her sanity for her, stopping her from falling into an almost unconscious state of bliss. She wanted to remember this look of his forever. She wanted to savour the moment.

Heavy lidded, he looked at her body and then back to her face. She knew that right now he was incapable of speech.

She'd never felt more beautiful. More admired. More wanted. And she felt the power surge into her. She moved, slowly, tilting her head so her hair fell, twisting her hips so she rode him, watching him imprisoned by passion beneath her.

But then her attempt to keep in control failed and animal instinct took over. She moved, keeping the feel of him so delicious, and the tension drove her, making her work harder, faster until she suddenly stopped, locked into sensation. He took over, gripping her hips, moving only that little bit more to knock them both over the edge, to those timeless moments of brilliant darkness where muscles jerked and pleasure pulsed through every part of her.

His arms held her close. With supreme effort she lifted her head and looked at him—saw the lazy mix of satisfaction and humour, and madly her desire lurched into life again. She couldn't stop herself seeking his kiss. And with a sinking heart she knew the only person she'd succeeded in trapping was herself.

CHAPTER TEN

THE next day Bella left Owen's arms again, using all her will power. 'I have a party on this afternoon. I have to get ready.'

She showered quickly, towel-dried her hair and then slipped into her underwear. She plugged in her hair curler.

'A fairy always needs her wand.' She grinned at Owen, who was still lying in bed but watching through the open doorway. She took a length of her hair and wound it round the rod. A few seconds later she released it and there was a bouncy curl. She did a few more, and then tied long sparkly ribbons into it.

'You really go the whole hog.' He'd rolled to his side, rested his head on his hand and was watching her every move.

She tilted her head, frowning at her reflection. 'I'm in character. I have to look the part, fulfil the fantasy for the child.'

'The perfect party princess.'

'Oh, no,' she corrected. 'I'm not the princess. The princess is the little girl whose birthday it is. I'm the fairy godmother, there to grant the wishes.'

She started work on her face. 'That's why I'm not in pink—that's their colour. I'm in silver and blue. I have pink wings for the girls, pink wands, tiaras. They get a unicorn tattoo and some glitter gel and then become part of the fairy princess network. I'm just there to help them tap into their imaginations.' She paused. 'Most of them don't even need me really.' Smoothing the glitter down her cheekbone, she paused. 'But there's always one. The shy one, the self-conscious one, the one who feels like she doesn't fit in.'

'So how do you get her to fit in?'

'That's always the challenge.' She smiled. 'Take it easy, gently. It can be hard when, for the others, you need to be effervescent. But I want to try to do it because I just know that inside she really wants to be up there and part of it all.'

'How do you know?'

She turned from the mirror. 'Because that was me,' she said simply. 'I was the self-conscious one.'

His eyes said, Yeah, right. So did his voice. 'I can't believe you were ever self-conscious.'

She smiled in triumph then. 'And that's how I know I'll make it as an actress.' One day. 'I'm good at pretending.'

She turned back to her pots of powder and paint. 'At the end of the day you just want them to have fun.'

'All I ever wanted was the food.' He burrowed back down in the bed.

'Figures.' She concentrated on her eyes, worked in silence for several minutes.

'Do you do boys' parties?' he asked.

At that she slanted him a look, saw the mischief in his face.

He tried to deny it, raising his hands all innocent-like. 'I'm serious. You're missing out on half your market.'

'I do. But admittedly it's more girls' parties than boys'. But there are often boys there—especially the preschooler ones. I have a pirate queen routine that I do for them.'

'You're a pirate?' He was back up on his elbows.

'I make a really good balloon sword.'

'You do?'

She giggled.

'The depth of your talent never ceases to amaze me,' he drawled, then watched her majestic nose wrinkle.

'Yeah right.'

She stood in front of the mirror, clad only in bra and panties, and he was having a hard time concentrating on stringing more than two words together.

'Where is the unicorn going today?'

'Where do you think it should go?' She grinned.

He knew exactly where it should go. On the slope of one of those creamy breasts, where it would peek out from the ruffles of the silver-and-blue dress, drawing the eye to the treasure beneath—not that his eyes needed any more pointers.

She glanced at the clock and gave a little squeal of horror. 'Stop distracting me. Lie there and be quiet. I can't be late.'

He didn't stay lying down but he did stay quiet. He stood, wrapped a towel round his hips to try to be a little decent, and then came right up behind her to watch more closely while she finished her make-up. Silently he studied her as she fixed the tattoo with a damp flannel, as she smoothed glitter gel across her shoulders and chest.

Her eyes met his in the mirror for a moment, then they skittered away, then back once more. He felt his tension—his everything—rising. He needed to know it was the same for her, this crazy, unfettered lust. He drew a breath and blew lightly over her shoulder, down onto the spot below her collarbone where the unicorn tattoo was drying. She shivered. He watched her nipples poke harder against the lace of her bra and he was about to pounce. But speedily she turned, left his space, went into the wardrobe where her dress was hanging. All too soon it was on and zipped and she was walking away.

'Right.' Her voice was high-pitched. 'See you later, then.'

He said nothing, just walked beside her all the way to the door, barely curbing his frustration.

As she reached to open it he reached for her—slid his hand round the nape of her neck, fingers wide so they caught in the curls of her hair. He pulled her to him for a hard, brief, melting kiss that didn't relieve him one iota.

'Later.' He basically growled.

He prowled around the apartment like a caged animal. Wished like hell he'd had her before she went to the damn party. But she'd been insistent on getting there on time. Now, three hours later, he was at bursting point. He'd never known a passion as intense as this. Never known a woman who could take up so much of his brain space either. He thought of her all the damn time. Thought up things he could do for her. Crazy stuff, silly stuff, irresistible stuff. He didn't much like it. Wanted to burn it out—blow it out with one big, hard puff.

Finally he heard the slam of the door downstairs. He went to the top of the stairs and waited. She was trotting up them, the silver fairy dress floating up towards him. His body tightened harder with her every step closer. He was filled with the urge to reach out and grab, to hold onto her in complete caveman style. He wanted to possess. He wanted to brand.

She got to the top and raised her brows as she saw him standing there. He watched the smokiness enter her eyes as she got his unspoken message. He watched as her breathing didn't ease at all—accelerated, in fact.

He took her arm and pulled her inside. The door shut behind them but he hardly heard it because by then he'd got his mouth on hers and he was asking for everything. She opened for him immediately and the rush of need overwhelmed him. He had to have her right now; he couldn't reclaim anything until he did.

He got them as far as the big table, pushed her against it, kissing her deeply while yanking up her dress. He pulled her panties out of the way while with his other hand he undid his jeans.

Her hands were in his hair and she leaned back, kissing him, taking him with her. He broke the seal of their lips briefly, to breathe and to thrust and then he was there and she was wet and hot and moving beneath him, full of life and heat and making him so welcome with a sigh and a murmur of delight. And then there was nothing because he kissed her again—hard and long and fierce while he possessed her with his body, pressing her against the hard wood. Trapping her, claiming her as the passion he had for her trapped and claimed him. He wanted to fight it, but pushed harder against her, into her. Harder and harder until suddenly there was everything bursting through him—colour and light and heat and the taste of her pleasure.

And then there was nothing.

He lifted his head, looked down at her and felt the tinge of embarrassment and guilt as he saw her bruised lips and the dazed look in her eyes. He'd just taken her rough and ready on his table, she still had her dress on, they were still joined and already he was tightening with anticipation about their next encounter.

He still wanted her. *How* he wanted her. He couldn't get enough.

Irritation, self-disgust, flared. Just sex. That was all this could be.

But just now had been more intense than anything. And here he was doing things, wanting things, thinking things… and it was madness because he knew, ultimately, he couldn't see this through. He didn't *want* complicated. He didn't want to be committed.

Her gaze ducked from his. She pushed gently at his shoulders. He left the warm embrace and instantly felt cold.

'The party was good, thanks.' She'd pulled up her knickers and was walking to the kitchen.

He grunted then, unable to stop the spurt of laughter bubbling through his annoyance.

'I think I've got another booking.'

He leaned on the table and tried to get his breath back, watching her as she moved around, completely at home in his kitchen. He needed to back out of this, but instead he walked over to her, ran a gentle hand down her arm. Quelled the urge to pull her back into his embrace. 'Are you OK?' he asked. Self-conscious wasn't really him. But it was flushing through, heating his cheeks now.

She looked surprised.

'I'm sorry, that was a little—'

'Barbarian?' she suggested.

He smiled again, still a little uncertain.

She put her glass down and a naughty twinkle lit her face. 'You can ravish me any time, Owen, you know that.'

He did know it. She welcomed him any time, every time. That didn't mean he should take advantage of her. Not any more. Guilt ripped through him. It trebled when he saw the tinge of vulnerability suddenly shadow her eyes. He'd got himself into a mess.

This was why he didn't do live-in anything. This was why he was better off alone. He just didn't have it in him to be the kind of guy a woman like Bella needed—any woman needed. He couldn't promise that he'd be there through thick and thin, or that he'd even *see* the thin patches. He sure as hell hadn't with his parents.

He didn't want to become bored and careless, as he had

with Liz. He didn't want to wake one day and see the lust in Bella's eyes had been replaced with disappointment and bitterness. And he definitely didn't want to be there to see her turn from his arms to someone else's.

His whole body clenched. It was time to push away. It was way beyond time, because it'd hurt—until now he hadn't realised it would. But better now than further along when it would only hurt more.

Then he thought of something else. Something so painful it twisted inside, becoming bitter anger. 'Bella, I didn't use anything just then. I didn't have a condom on.'

He'd just lost it. Seen her. Kissed her. Taken her as fast as possible. And now—what if? He could hardly bear to look at her. He already knew he'd make a lousy father.

Bella carefully kept her weight back against the bench; her legs still weren't working properly and at the expression in his eyes they were going even weaker. But it wasn't from lust. It was from fear. Because it was fear she could read in his eyes. Fear and regret.

'I know.' She'd had the thought in her head for a split second, but it had gone as she'd been swept away in the chaos and bliss of the moment.

'You didn't stop me.' His eyes had narrowed.

'You didn't stop yourself,' she reminded him. She'd wanted it as much as he had—and he had *wanted* it. She'd never seen that expression on his face before—that naked need. The desire that he could scarcely seem to control. It had turned her on— for a moment she'd felt nothing but power and then she too had been totally lost. But he still wasn't willing to recognise the strength of it. Right now he looked as if he wanted to run.

'Is there a chance you might...' He didn't even seem able to say it.

'Have a baby?' She wanted to use the b-word. Not just say pregnant. She wanted to see how he'd react to the mental image of a tiny little life—real. A child that shared their blood, that breathed because of them.

The loss of colour in his cheeks was almost imperceptible, but she was watching closely.

His 'Yeah' was drawn out and low.

'There's a chance.' It was a slim chance, very slim as her period was due in only a day or two. But she wasn't ready to let him off the hook just yet. She was hurt from that look, the dread and fear in it. And she wanted to know what it was he was going to say.

He exhaled. 'Whatever happens, you know I'll support you.' His gaze slid from hers. 'Whatever you decide.'

Whatever *she* decided? So it would be her choice and hers alone. He wanted no part in anything that might be? She squeezed her fingers hard on the bench behind her. Still said nothing, but only because her heart was ripping.

'Whatever you want to do,' he was mumbling now. 'I don't…'

What, he didn't—mind? *Care?*

She'd known, hadn't she? He'd told her that very first night. And, no matter what she fantasised, the reality was exactly as he'd told it. She'd been warned.

But she hadn't paid attention—had just had the bit between her teeth and gone along for the ride. And the consequences were going to be more serious than she'd ever thought possible.

She'd never had her heart broken before.

So much for independence. She'd gone and got herself totally dependent on someone who could never offer her anything like all that she wanted. She wished he'd go away and she could lick her wounds in private. Regroup. Gather up her shredded pride. But at that her pride came racing back, fully armed.

She crossed the room, picked up the little bag she'd dropped by the door and thanked the heavens that the family today had paid her in cash. She opened the envelope and flung the dollar notes down on the bench next to Owen.

'What's that for?' He looked at it, distaste all over his face.

'That's the money for rent, for the four new tyres that Bubbles has—don't think I haven't noticed them—for the petrol, for the groceries, for all the dinners, the wine, for the website and for the hotel bill in Waiheke.' She stopped for breath. It wasn't nearly enough to cover all that, but it sure felt good to say it.

'I don't want it,' he said flatly.

'I won't have you paying for things for me.' She tossed her head. 'It makes me feel like a who—'

'Don't you dare!' he shouted then, his step closer shutting her up. Anger flushed his cheeks and flashed in his eyes. 'I have *never* paid for sex, Bella, and I don't intend to start now.'

'Really?' she said scornfully, sounding a whole lot braver than she felt. 'But isn't that what's happening here?'

'You know damn well it isn't.' He spoke through his teeth. 'It's just money. It's meaningless.'

Like the sex? Not to her, it wasn't.

He seemed to read her face and growled. 'Why are you so damn keen to label everything?'

'Why are you so keen to deny everything?' The attraction between them wasn't anything ordinary—surely he could sense that?

'This is just sex, Bella.' His words came like the cracks of a whip. 'I like it. You like it. That's all there is to it.'

Bella blinked. Bit the inside of her cheek as she absorbed

the shock of what he'd said and the depth of his scowl. Humiliation started to seep into her very core.

'Why did you pay for that night in the hotel?' She winced. Did he hear that slight cry in her voice?

'I don't know,' he answered irritably, stepping away. 'It was just a spur-of-the-moment thing. I knew you were tight for money. I just wanted to help you out.'

'Well, I don't want your help.' She spoke quickly, marched to the bedroom, unzipping her dress and walking right out of it, leaving it on the floor. She'd never be able to wear it again without thinking of this moment—the time when he'd taken her so passionately and then turned on her.

'Don't you?' He was right behind her. 'Well, you're certainly not helping yourself.'

'What does that mean?' Furious with the way she felt tears close by, she picked a skirt and pulled on the nearest top she could find.

'You won't let me help you. You won't let anyone help you.'

'That's right, Owen. I won't.' She grabbed a flannel and scrubbed her face hard, blocking the sight and sound of him with water from the tap, stopping any stupid tears from even starting.

When her face was bare and reddened, but masked once more, she turned and headed for the door.

'Where are you going?'

'I have an audition.'

'Now?'

She sent him a glare while slipping into her sandals. 'Yes, now.'

'And you're going like that?'

'Yes.' She walked.

He swore. 'You deliberately sabotage yourself.'

After a minuscule pause she kept walking.

'You do,' he said, seemingly just getting into the swing of getting at her. 'You spend over an hour getting ready for one of your parties and less than five minutes getting ready for an audition that could change your life. It's like you don't really want it.'

She whirled to face him. 'Of course I want it.'

'No, you don't! You're never late to work at the café and yet you're late almost every time to a casting call. Tell me,' he said snidely. 'What do you believe in, Bella? Fairies?' He bent to pick up her dress from the floor, his acidity eating an even bigger hole in her heart. 'Do you really think you've got some fairy godmother who's going to make it all happen for you?'

'Of course not.' She turned back and started walking to the door again.

'Then what do you believe in?'

She said nothing, kept walking. It didn't seem like the moment to mention luck.

'Why don't you try believing in yourself?' he called after her. 'If *you* don't believe in your abilities, why should anyone else?'

She couldn't not face that. He was in the middle of the room, shaking his head at her. 'Instead you blame anything you can. Your family isn't supportive, you haven't had formal acting training, you haven't had that "lucky" break. But it's not about luck, it's about making the decision to do it and then persevering, putting in that hard work.'

Her anger rose another notch. 'I work damn hard.'

'I know, but not at—'

'But nothing,' she snapped. 'You don't know the first thing about acting, about going to casting call after casting call. It's not about learning the lines and spouting them automaton fashion. There *is* luck involved. Who's your competition?

What look are they after? You have to be in the right place at the right time with the right product. I haven't yet.'

'Then you keep going,' he lectured, her dress hanging from his hands. 'You research. You find out what they want and you give it to them as professionally as you can. You believe and work and eventually it'll happen.'

'You make it all sound so easy,' she said bitterly. 'Like it's some computer program.'

'I know it's not easy. But you have to believe in yourself. You have to have the passion for it.'

'I do have the passion!' She was yelling now. 'God, Owen, what do you want?'

'This isn't about what I want!' he yelled back. 'This is about you and you're not the person you can be yet. You're floating along the edges too scared to dive right in. I don't think you even know what it is you *do* want. It's much easier to skate along and blame it all on everyone or anything else.'

'Well, what about you?' The viciousness of his attack forced her into fight mode. Red-hot anger ran through her veins, releasing the words from her. 'You're not exactly living life to the full either, are you, Mr Workaholic? And as for this Mr Don't-Get-Near-Me-Because-I'm-Selfish routine… What sort of a rubbish excuse is that, Owen? You're not selfish. Doling out money *proves* you're not selfish,' she shouted, losing her grip entirely. 'What you are is scared!'

His face whitened, his jaw locked, but she hardly noticed. She was on way too much of a roll now.

'You say you don't want labels, but you're the one trying to squeeze us into the smallest compartment possible. Sex is all it is, huh? Well, how convenient for you. You can just keep your distance and don't have to invest anything remotely risky like emotion or take responsibility. What is it you're afraid of,

Owen?' Scathing, she flung him the answer. 'Failing at something for once in your life? Hell, I fail at things all the time, but at least I have the guts to get back up and give it another go.'

She spat her fury and hurt. 'So don't you dare lecture me about hovering on life's edges. You're the one not facing up to what's really going on here. You're the coward!'

Breathless, she stopped, realising what she'd said and all she'd revealed—the degree to which she was involved, how much she wanted more, how she wanted him to accept that there *was* more…but, oh, my Lord, maybe there really wasn't anything more in this for him? Of course there wasn't—she wasn't anything like the kind of woman he'd really want. She turned, more desperate to get out of there than ever before.

'Who's the coward now?' he roared after her. 'Who's the one throwing the accusations and then walking out without giving me a chance to respond?'

She whirled back, bleeding inside. 'Well, what's the point in my staying just to hear you deny everything and say nothing?' Bitterly, she glared at him.

His hands were fisted in her dress, rumpling it so bad it would have to go back to the dry-cleaners again. His face was still pale and a picture of savage tension. He met her glare with one of his own—just as bitter, just as furious. But his jaw was clamped and as she stared she could see his muscles flex down tighter.

He had no answer to that and she didn't want to hear it anyway. She stalked out of the apartment and slammed the door as hard as she could. It was all so easy for him. He was nothing but killer instinct. Nothing but what he wanted now, now, now. All 'I want that, I'm going to do that…' and off he went and had and did with no regard to consequences. It would serve him right to suffer the consequences for once.

Because she was. She couldn't compartmentalise this the way he wanted to—this *thing* was all too big, for her anyway.

She fumed all the way to the audition and barely noticed the competition. She was too busy stewing over the argument. Too busy trying to stay mad and not recognise the extent of the break in her heart.

They had to call her name twice.

CHAPTER ELEVEN

BELLA spent that night alone in the spare room, most of it awake, plotting her way out of there. She was mortified at what Owen had said and what she'd said—and spent hours deciding on the truth of it all. This was just sex for him, and his efforts to help her out—the dress, the website, the way he cooked her dinner—was simply him. He'd stop and help an old lady cross the street—that didn't mean he was on his way to falling in love with her.

She was such a fool. And that was the point, wasn't it? She was such a klutz he couldn't help himself trying to help her. Because that was the kind of guy he was. And now she'd humiliated herself completely by insisting that there was more to it. Of course he hadn't been able to reply—he hadn't wanted to hurt her, and he'd already spelt it out as plainly as he could: sex, that was all there was to it.

'How'd it go?'

Damn. She'd hoped he'd have gone downstairs to work already this morning. Instead he was sitting at the table. She felt her cheeks warm at the sight of it. Truthfully, she'd forgotten about the audition the minute she'd walked out of it. Somehow the lines had come to her. She must have come across like an automaton. Ah, well, chalk another one up to experience.

'Don't ask.'

He looked moody. 'I'm sorry I was so grumpy.'

'I'm sorry I was so ungrateful.' She inched closer. 'I really appreciate everything you've done for me, Owen.' Oh, God, this was awkward.

'It's nothing.' He shook his head. 'No trouble.'

That was right—not for him. 'Please let me pay back what I owe you.'

His expression tightened more. 'It's just money, Bella. It doesn't matter.'

'It matters to me.' She hated being in his debt like this. Hated that all she had to offer in return was her heart, and he'd never want that.

'OK.' He paused, stared hard at the table. 'But only if you stay. I'd like you to stay.' He paused. 'Just until you get yourself sorted.'

There it was, the caveat. She'd been right—he couldn't hold back the offer of assistance, but nor could he offer anything else. Now she felt too awkward to say yes, too awkward to say no.

'OK.' Her reply came out on a heavy sigh. She couldn't see that getting herself sorted was going to happen any time soon, but she'd be out of here regardless. She took a deep breath and tackled the most awkward bit of all. 'I'll tell you as soon as I know.' A few days to be certain, then she'd leave. She refused to think about what would happen if she was pregnant—that was altogether too scary.

He looked back at her, looking as sombre as she'd sounded. She knew he knew what she was referring to. And she knew how badly he didn't want it.

The next two days dragged for Owen. He'd wanted to back off, but only seemed to be digging himself in deeper. He kept reliving that argument. She'd touched a nerve and he'd flared up at her, but he hadn't said anything that wasn't true—had he? He couldn't help the sickening feeling that he'd thrown something precious away before he'd even realised he had it.

Worse, he had the feeling she'd been the one hitting truth on the head at the end there. He couldn't face it—couldn't face her, until he knew whether she was pregnant or not. He couldn't *think* until he knew. It was like waiting for a jury to return its verdict—were they going to get a life sentence? Either way there'd be guilt and bitterness. And it was worse than Liz—this time he was to blame. It hadn't been Bella's fault at all. The sooner it was all over, the better.

And yet he missed her. How he missed her. He practically had to lock himself into his bedroom to stop from going into hers. His arms ached with emptiness. Sleep was utterly elusive—and so was she. She worked long hours at the café and hid in her room the rest of the time. He spent more time in the offices downstairs to give them both some space.

But truly finding space was impossible while she was staying with him. And he wasn't ready to ask her to leave yet. He still wanted her with a passion that was tearing him up inside and, more than that, he wanted to make things *right*. He decided a trip away was the answer. Just a couple of days. Regain perspective and work out what the hell he was going to do if she was pregnant.

She hadn't mentioned it again. Whereas by now Liz had chosen names and been practically putting the baby on the list for the most exclusive schools. Bella was making no demands—making a point of it, in fact. She'd backed right off and had shut down her expressive face. He hated that too— he wished he knew what she was thinking and wanted to know if she was OK.

* * *

Owen had withdrawn from her. He was working later, not coming into the café any more. Bella munched on her small bowl of muesli and watched him pack his laptop into his case.

'How long are you gone for?'

'I'm not sure yet. Couple of days maybe, I don't know.'

She nodded.

'You've got the security code?'

She nodded again. She'd take the opportunity to find herself a new flat. She could move into a flat-share with some students. There'd be plenty of cheap ones out in the suburbs. That was her plan. This was the end of the end. She knew it. He knew it.

He glanced into the contents of her bowl and his cheeky smile appeared. She hadn't seen it for a while and it made her heart ache.

'You're supposed to eat that stuff in the morning, you know.'

She managed a wry grin back. 'Better late than never.'

Both their grins faded.

Owen listened to the flight announcements, took another sip of his coffee, gripped his bag that little bit tighter. He should have checked in by now. If he didn't check in within the next minute or so he'd miss his flight. He looked into his cup—he still had half of it to go. It would be a shame to throw away good airport coffee.

Bella hadn't said anything. She'd known he was running away—he could see the reflection of his eyes in hers and knew she saw the truth of it there. But still she was making no demands.

And wasn't that what he thought he always wanted? No demands? For fear he wouldn't be able to meet them? Because he wasn't willing to provide the emotional support someone else needed? Damn it, Bella didn't seem to want *any* kind of support. And suddenly it was all he wanted to do. He wanted to know if she was OK, if she was scared or secretly excited or desperately unhappy. He wanted to help her deal with however she was feeling. And he wanted her to help *him* too.

His heart jerked. Maybe she didn't demand because she simply didn't care. He knew that for a lie. He saw it in her eyes. Every time she'd taken him into her she'd been loving him. Just sex? What a joke.

This time, he couldn't walk away. This time, he didn't want to.

The taxi seemed to take for ever. Driving alongside the water, the lights reflected on it. The aeroplanes looked as if they were going to end up in the sea if they didn't slam the brakes on damn fast. Was that him? Headed for a drowning if he didn't skid to a halt soon?

The apartment was in darkness and for an awful moment he thought she'd gone. Then he saw the large lump on the floor. He flicked on the lights. She was huddled in her beanbag. He took in her pale face, her eyes large and bruised and startled.

'I'm sorry, I didn't mean to scare you.' He put his bag on the table.

She blinked, clearly gathering her wits. 'What happened?'

'Last-minute change of plan.' He paused, inventing a non-excuse. 'I managed to get out of it.'

'Oh.'

He could see her biting back other questions and felt bad because of it. He wanted to answer her, wanted to communicate—a little at least.

He stripped off his jacket, wondering why the hell he was so buttoned up in a suit. It had all been for the show of it. He went to the bench in search of wine.

'I'm not pregnant.' Her voice was low, matter-of-fact. It took a few moments to register what she'd actually told him.

Not pregnant. No baby.

He was glad he was against the bench because he needed its strength for a second. He'd never expected to feel it as a blow. Never expected to feel *disappointment*. Only now was he seeing it in his mind, her body rounded with a baby, and then holding a child, his child. The ache that opened up in him was terrifying.

'When did you find out?' He managed to sound almost normal as he poured a large glass of red.

'Just tonight.'

He nodded, took a big sip. 'You're feeling OK?'

'Oh, sure. Fine.' She mirrored his nod.

He searched her pale features again and knew she was faking it. She looked miserable. He saw the half-eaten cake of chocolate beside her. For a mad moment he wanted to sweep her into his arms and tell her not to be sad, that they'd make babies together any time she wanted to. She just had to say the word.

But he didn't. He took a breath, another sip of wine and a long minute to regain sanity. He still felt lousy. Why—when this was what he wanted, right? No encumbrances.

'Want to watch a movie?' He walked over to her, touched her shoulder gently. Instantly felt a bit better. 'You can choose.'

'I already have.'

Then he noticed the blinking of the screen—black and white. *Casablanca*. Again.

'Need anything else—ice cream? Wine?'

'Yes, please.'

* * *

What she really wanted was a hug. What she really wanted was to know his reaction. At least he wasn't doing back-flips and saying, 'Thank God, what a relief.' She didn't know if she could handle that. Because even though she'd been fighting for independence for so long, the thought of a baby had intrigued her—because it would be his. She'd even lain awake and wondered whether their child would have his brilliant blue eyes or her pale ones. But he wasn't giving anything away.

She decided to find out. She took the wine he offered, and was surprised to see her hand wasn't shaking. 'With your attitude to marriage there's no need to ask. I know you're relieved.'

'I…'

'It's OK, Owen. You don't have to hide it.'

He looked away from her, as if what she'd said had hurt. 'I haven't got what they need.' His voice was low. 'Children deserve more than an emotionally absent father.'

She frowned. Emotionally absent? Owen wasn't absent—he was more real, more vital than anyone she'd ever met. She could see the trouble inside him on his face—something was stirring in him and she didn't think it was altogether because of her. But what? And she remembered what he'd said—what his ex had said—that he was selfish. Why had the woman thought that? What had happened? When it was obvious he was generous, not just financially but in more ways than he'd admit. Suddenly Bella wanted him to see that.

'Who waters your garden, Owen?'

He frowned.

'Your plants upstairs,' she explained.

'What's that got to do with anything?'

'Everything.' She smiled. 'That's noticing, that's remembering, that's caring.' She paused. 'That's all that children need.'

He was shaking his head. 'No,' he said. 'They also need to be wanted.'

Her suspicions solidified as she heard his desolate hollowness. And even though the thought of the answer terrified her, she couldn't stop from asking the question. 'Have you been through this before, Owen?'

Owen owed her honesty. Then she'd see the person he really was, and this whole ending thing wouldn't be nearly so bad—she'd be out of his place in no time. Because no woman would understand the way he'd reacted—especially not one who liked kids so much she actually worked with them. It would be over, and he could move on. 'You know I had that girlfriend, right?'

'The one who said you were selfish.'

'Right.' He grinned without mirth. 'Around the time I was selling the company she told me she was pregnant.'

Bella nodded.

He looked away from her, not coping with the hint of sympathy he saw in her eyes. 'I wasn't remotely keen. I felt nothing. I felt worse than nothing.' He took a breath and said it. 'I didn't want it. How terrible is that? Not to want your own flesh and blood?' He'd felt trapped. He still felt guilty about that.

'She was dreaming up names and was all excited and hanging out for a ring and I didn't want to know a thing about it.' He'd withdrawn and gone remote on her rather than admitting how he felt. Certainly hadn't dropped down on one knee instantly as she'd seemed to expect he would. 'It was a crazy time. I was working all hours negotiating this deal…' That was no excuse; he should have been just a little more interested. But the fact was he'd been wanting out of the relationship for a while already. He just hadn't got round to breaking off with her—too busy to be bothered. And he was still too busy to be able to think it through properly—he'd just avoided the issue for a while. Tried to pretend it wasn't real, tried to swallow the guilt that came with that.

'What happened?'

'She was mistaken. There was no baby.' She'd been late, that was all. When she'd told him, with red-rimmed eyes and a catch in her throat, he'd been so relieved and he hadn't been able to hide it from her. That was when she'd lost it—screamed at him about how selfish he was, how unsupportive, that his heart only beat for his business. And she'd been right. He hadn't wanted her or the baby or any of it. It had got really ugly then, and in the course of the argument Liz had slipped up.

It wasn't that she'd been late at all. She'd made it up—there had never been the possibility of a pregnancy. She'd tried to manipulate him—cornering him just as he was about to come into vast wealth. And she'd done it in such a low fashion— because even though he'd known it probably wouldn't work, his integrity would have insisted that he try. He'd have married her and she knew it. It was just that he hadn't come to the party soon enough for her to get away with it. Whether she'd wanted him or the money he didn't know—he suspected the latter.

He'd been viciously angry then and vowed never to be put in the same position again. No woman would wield that threat over him. He didn't want it—marriage, babies—not ever.

'She met someone else not long after.' He dragged out a cynical smile, feeling sorry for the poor bastard she'd netted. 'She married him, has a kid or two. She's happy.' She'd got what she'd wanted.

And he was happy too, right? Happy with his choices and with his freedom to focus on his work and on fun.

The silence was long. Bella was looking at him, expression

clouded. He felt bad—the bitterness that Liz had left him with wasn't for her. This hadn't been her fault—it had been his irresponsibility. He'd broken his own rules, he hadn't played safe—and he should have stopped fooling with her a week ago.

'I'm sorry, Bella.' He met her gaze squarely. 'I should never have put you in danger.' He didn't want to treat her badly, and he probably would have.

'I put myself there too, remember?' She looked away, stood. 'I think I'll go to bed. I'm a bit tired.'

He stood too. 'You OK? Comfortable? Need a painkiller or anything?'

She shook her head, a sad smile twisting her lips. He knew what she was wondering—if he felt the same about this baby-that-wasn't, if he had the same antipathy towards the idea. But he couldn't answer her, couldn't bear to think on it because it was hurting him more than he'd ever thought it could. And what hurt more was the realisation that she'd been right. He was a coward.

He watched her go. For the first time feeling as if he'd missed out on everything.

It had started out as the party from hell. The house had been tiny. The wind had meant there was no way they could be outside. The stereo system had failed. And there had been the most hideous boyfriend of one of the mothers who'd hit on Bella before she'd even got all the way up the path.

She'd worked hard to turn it around for the poor kid. Wished the audience of adults would just go away so she could have some fairy fun with the wee ones. In the end it had been good old-fashioned bubbles that had saved it—as she'd made big ones they'd spotted the rainbows in them. And then she'd read them the tale of the unicorn and the temporary tattoos had come out and the face paints and the magic of make-believe.

Bella parked Bubbles in the garage and braced herself. The week had gone quickly and she still hadn't moved out. Still hadn't the strength to leave the man she ached to love.

Now, with the payment from this party, she had no more excuses. She could give him at least some of the money she owed and get out. She'd phone her father for the rest to start afresh. It was best, because now she'd thought about it, she knew she wanted the whole marriage and kids bit. She couldn't live with less. So she needed to get away and over him.

He wasn't waiting to pounce on her the minute she walked back in. Instead he lifted his head from the paper he was reading in his big chair, took one look and frowned at her.

'Didn't it go so good?'

She sighed. 'It was OK. But the house was tiny—and I mean tiny. And they'd invited twelve kids and all their parents were there.'

It made her skin itchy just thinking about it—all that close contact with complete strangers. The kids were OK. It was the adults who grossed her out. And she simply couldn't perform to her best in an environment like that.

He shoved his paper to the floor and stood. 'Actually I've been thinking about you and your parties.' He paused, then words seemed to tumble from him. 'Why don't you use some of the space downstairs? You could do it up and get all the kids to come here. It would save you from lecherous uncles.'

Bella stared at him. 'You're kidding, right?' He'd never want that—would he?

'No. It might as well be used for something. It'll get other prospective tenants off my back and it'll only be used part of the time. During the week when my guys are in upstairs it'll be quiet.'

'Isn't it a waste of your resource?'

'It's mine to waste.' He shrugged. 'And it'll only be part of it. Still room for a restaurant if I ever want one.'

Oh, my, she thought as he winked. That sparkle was back and his expression was lighter and Bella felt herself falling once more, mesmerised by his vibrancy.

'I'd have to decorate it,' she said, half dazed. 'I don't have the money.'

'I'll loan you. Start-up costs. You can pay me back once you're up and running. You'll make it back in no time.'

She shook her head, stopped thinking completely. This was crazy.

'Bella.' He stepped near her. 'This is what you're good at. This is what you love. Every time you do a party you come home with bookings for at least one or two more. You're a wonderful entertainer. This is what you're meant to do.'

The idea was so tempting. Her own party space. She'd never even thought of it before. And she'd have such fun designing the venue… Unstoppable ideas swirled through her head.

He was grinning at her, as if he knew.

She inhaled deeply, shook her head. 'Owen, I can't.'

'Why not?'

Because things were complicated between them. She didn't want this to be his latest idea that he'd set up and then skip on to the next. They weren't together any more—were they? She really needed to get over him and on with her life. 'I need to get out and find a new flat. I can't stay here for ever.'

There was another non-committal shrug. 'Maybe, but there's plenty of time for that. Why not focus on building a business first? You could do the food too, couldn't you?'

Of course she could—standing on her head. More ideas teased her—of menus and fun things and dreams and fantasies.

'Tell you what.' He kept talking. 'Why don't you just take a segment downstairs and paint it? See what you think. It might not be right as there isn't an outdoor area. It might not work out at all.'

But it would work out. No outdoors didn't matter, not if she created a grotto indoors. And she knew she could do that. And if they built a pirate ship the kids could climb up it and hunt for treasure and…and…

She looked at him. He was acting so casually about this. And yet, in his own way, he was pushing it. Batting away her arguments with a shrug and his usual 'of course you can' attitude. What was his real agenda? Was there anything more to this than a simple offer of help?

Her mind—and heart—leapt to the most blissful conclusion. Was this his way of keeping her in his life? On the terms that he could handle?

Probably not, she scoffed at herself. This was just his latest obsession. And once it was set up he'd be onto something else. She was looking everywhere for anything. But the little bubble of hope wouldn't be popped. She'd keep on hoping, keep on dreaming. Maybe, just maybe, he'd wake up to the fact that there was more between them than either of them could have imagined. Or was it just her imagination going overtime again?

'Come on, let's go look at it now.' He took her arm, half dragging her down the stairs. The space was huge.

'We could partition it off.' He stood, arms stretched out marking imaginary walls.

'I'd have to get consents.' Her trailing footsteps echoed. 'There'd be building work to be done. I'd have to buy so much stuff.'

'Yeah, but wouldn't it be great?' His eyes were shining so damn attractively. No wonder he was successful—he could make anyone believe in anything. Passionate, enthusiastic, energetic.

'Look—' he dragged her over to one corner '—you could have a little shop next door here selling things—like the fairy dresses and the tattoos and glittery stuff. And you could paint a mural—throw in a few tigers.'

She was amazed. 'You've really thought about this.'

'Sure.'

She could have different themed parties—art, beading, pirates, jungles, teddy bears' picnics—the list was endless. His enthusiasm infected her—bubbling through her veins.

'Owen.' She was shaking her head, but she couldn't stop the smile.

He smiled back at her. And then he stepped closer, his hands on her arms. She only needed to take a step forward to touch him—and she wanted to touch him so much.

'Think about it,' he said softly.

She was. She read the offer deep within him. On a plate he was handing her everything she could ever want—anything material. But what she really wanted wasn't a tangible thing. And he didn't think he had it to give. But he did—and so badly she wanted him to give it to *her.* She was a fool, such a fool, but his blue eyes shone even more brilliantly and she couldn't ever say no—not when he looked at her like that.

He whispered again. 'I'm going to kiss you, Bella. So if you don't want me to, you better speak up now.'

Pure, deep, hopeless longing overcame her, rendering her silent, waiting and so willing for whatever he wanted.

But it wasn't the fiercely passionate kiss she expected. It was soft and sweet and so gentle. He stepped closer, his hands lifting to frame her face—so tender. She felt her eyes prickle. She closed them quickly and the bliss simply increased. It rushed from both her toes and the tip of her head—meeting in the middle of her, expanding, taking over the beating of her heart.

Suddenly, somehow, they were on the floor and he'd rolled, pulling her on top, protecting her from the cold, dusty concrete.

'This is bad,' she breathed. 'This is where the kids will be playing.'

'No kids here now. Only a couple of adults. Consenting.'

'Oh, yes.'

CHAPTER TWELVE

BELLA was dusting the shelves at the café the next morning, mentally choosing paint colours, when she heard the beep of her mobile. She pulled it from her pocket. Didn't recognise the number. She didn't recognise the voice either—fortunately the woman said she was calling from Take One Agency....

Oh, God. The audition. Just over a week ago and frankly she'd forgotten it. It had been the day she'd had that massive argument with Owen.

'I'm pleased to be able to offer you the part of...'

Bella tuned out—entering shock. She was being offered a part on a national touring show.

'Rehearsals start in Christchurch next week...'

She'd be paid. A full-time job as an actress—in a musical theatre production. Excitement flooded through her. She couldn't believe it. Couldn't wait to get home and tell Owen.

Owen.

She pulled up short. Owen—who was probably designing her a pirate ship this very minute. Owen—who was probably the reason why she'd got the job in the first place. Owen—who had made her so mad she'd gone into that audition all guns blazing and uncaring of the consequences. Owen—who had never made fun of her parties, but who made everything matter.

She had to leave him. Leave the business—while it was still a seed, just a fragment of a dream. For one wild moment she wanted to turn down the part. Pretend it hadn't happened. But as she listened to the woman warble on about the details she knew she couldn't. This was it, her shot at the big time. Do well in this and she could springboard to other, bigger, better shows.

Sydney, London, New York… Her imagination ballooned.

But there was Owen. And she wanted Owen. And she'd thought if she had a little more time, she might show Owen how much he had to offer—and not just in the money sense. But it probably was for the best, because that was the fantasy, wasn't it? Her winning him. She'd soon know anyway. She'd tell him about the part, see how he reacted. Then she'd know for sure if this was still just sex or something else entirely. She spent the afternoon totally excited, totally nervous, totally torn.

She raced home, but he wasn't there and she paced round the big space. Not sure how to tell him. How to act. But when he finally appeared the thrill, the disbelief, the pride all bubbled out of her.

'I got the part, I got the part!' She ran to him, her smile and arms wide.

He caught her, sweeping them both into the embrace, lifting and spinning her, grinning hugely.

'What part?' he asked when her toes touched the floor again.

'On the show.'

'What show?' He laughed.

'It's not the lead or anything,' she clarified. 'But it is a minor character. Well, quite a major minor character actually. And I do understudy the lead, which means in some matinees I'll be the lead.'

He was still laughing. 'This is fantastic. Which theatre? When?'

Her smile suddenly felt a little stiff. 'It's a travelling show.'

'Travelling?' His hands loosened.

She took her full weight, brushed a stray bit of hair back behind her ear and blurted it all. 'Rehearsals are in Christchurch. The show starts there and then tours. If the New Zealand tour is successful, then it'll go to Australia.'

'Wow.' He was still grinning as he stepped away. 'Wow.'

He went straight to the fridge and pulled out a bottle. 'This calls for a celebration, right?'

The cork fired right across the room, bubbles frothed. She watched as he poured, staring at the label. Good grief, she'd only ever seen that sort of champagne in the pages of posh magazines.

'Yeah,' she said slowly. Had he known a celebration was in order?

He handed her a glass. 'When do you go?'

'Later this week.'

'How long do you rehearse for?'

'Almost six weeks, I think. Then the tour starts. I don't know how long that'll be ultimately.'

He was all questions; she had no time to think of anything but the answers. It was a good twenty minutes before they quietened.

'You did it,' he said softly, smiling.

'I did.' She still couldn't believe it—any of it. Especially that she'd be leaving, right when things were getting interesting. She finally broached the subject. 'I'm really sorry about not using the space downstairs.'

'Oh. Don't worry about it. It was just an idea. I have lots of them.' He grinned.

Her heart ached. He really didn't mind.

'You'll have to phone and tell your family.'

She paused. 'Not yet.' She'd see how it went first—make sure it was a complete success that she could be proud of. And she was still nervous about contacting Vita. Her sister was too good at prying and she'd want to do a post-mortem over what had happened on Waiheke.

'This is great,' he said. 'This is really good.'

She supposed it was. An easy, clean finish for him. She'd been the one building dream castles. Seeing them shatter, hurt.

Owen could see the shadows entering her eyes and steeled himself not to give in. His heart was breaking—just as he'd found he had one. But he could not do it. He could see the question in her face and he refused to answer it. He was not going to give her the out. He was not going to hold onto her only to have her resent him for it in—what?—six months or a year's time. He was not going to ruin it for her.

She had to go. And she had to go utterly free of him. So he talked it up, went on about how exciting it was, how wonderful. She was finally going to realise her dreams. And not once did he mention how it was tearing him apart inside. Not once did he mention how much he wanted her to stay—to choose him. He gave her no choice. Because he knew that right now, inside, she cared for him. But she deserved to have her chance. For a moment there he'd thought they could have it all, but fate had decided it for both of them. The champagne tasted bitter. He'd put it in the fridge to celebrate something else entirely. He'd been going to cast off the coward label and embrace the risk—of emotion and responsibility—just as she'd challenged. Only now he was forced into a far more brave action—letting her go. The irony of it all really sucked.

Bella didn't take time off work. Nor did Owen. In some ways it was a relief. She worked the last two days at the café totally on auto. They had pizza one night, Thai the next. Before she knew it, it was the last night. She was flying. He'd insisted. Reckoned he'd got a cheap deal on the Internet. She'd let him. It beat the ferry and bus option. She was always sick on the ferry.

They'd talked and teased and joked their way through sex. And it had always been wonderful and fun. But this was no joke. She was making love to him for the last time and then she was leaving.

There was nothing she could say. There was no way of changing it—there was no time.

And so for the first time she caressed him in complete silence. Kissing and kissing and kissing so there was no chance to voice the secrets lodged in her heart. That she'd fallen in love with him. Wanted to be with him. Wanted to stay.

As he moved down her body she couldn't stop thinking. Couldn't quite give herself over to the lust. Couldn't enjoy it the way she really wanted to. He couldn't and wouldn't give her what she wanted. And what she wanted was taking her away. Acting was what she wanted most, right?

This was their last time—she had to make the most of it. But all she could think was that it *was* the last time. And that was ruining everything. She wanted to stop. She didn't want there to be a last time.

He must have known because he stopped nuzzling her breasts. Instead he lifted his head and looked in her eyes, framed her face with his hands—so gently. And then *he* kissed *her.* He kissed and kissed until she could no longer think. Until there was no room in her head for doubt or pain. Only touch.

And then, when her mind was gone and she was all sensation, he stroked the rest of her, leaning close so he could follow the path of his fingers with his eyes. He stroked and kissed and gently blew on her hot skin. Moving with such powerful gentleness it was almost her undoing. But he too was silent.

She closed her eyes against the message she so badly wanted to read in his and just let him play with her until the need for the ultimate satisfaction grew too strong for both of them.

When he entered her this time she held her breath, tightening around him, closing him into her embrace with her arms and legs and everything. In her head words had returned and she was chanting: not going to let you go, not going to let you go.

But she was the one going. And she didn't know if she really had the strength to follow through on it.

But later, as she dressed, alone in his bedroom, she knew she had to leave. It was to protect herself. She owed herself the chance of meeting her dreams. And she couldn't stay with a man who didn't want long term—not when she did. Marriage and babies were on her wish-list and she couldn't change that—just as she couldn't change him.

She tried to make the goodbye as quick as she could. It didn't dim the pain at all. She wouldn't look him in the face— couldn't. He wanted to take her to the airport, was insistent. It tore her up inside as he objected.

Finally she looked at him, unable to hide the ache. 'Please, Owen. Let me do this myself.'

He stopped then, a shadow passing over his face. 'You don't have to do everything yourself, Bella. It's OK to have help from people when you need it. Remember that, won't you?'

Yes, it was OK, but not all the time. And she had to do this alone; it was the only way she could.

The taxi was there in minutes and she turned to him feeling as if she had sawdust in her eyes and sandpaper in her throat. He lifted her bag into the boot.

'I'll call you,' he said.

'Actually—' she cleared her throat '—I'd rather you didn't.'

He stared at her.

She didn't want to be half hoping—*wholly* hoping—for the next however many months or years it was going to take to get over him. She needed it to end now. It was the perfect opportunity. Clean, final. Just how he'd like it. She didn't want him to pretend to offer anything else.

'You don't want me to contact you at all?'

She forced her head to move, slowly, side to side.

He stared at her for a long moment, ignoring the driver waiting patiently in the car.

'OK,' he said quietly. 'If that's what you want.'

She nodded then and looked down, not wanting to misread anything more in his face. Wanting to kill all her hope now. She didn't trust her voice at all.

There was a moment of silence. She knew she should move—the driver was waiting, the meter was ticking already. But all that moved were her lashes as she lifted her eyes, unable to resist one last long look at him. His eyes were still a brilliant blue, but charged with a variety of emotions—confusion? Regret?

She couldn't take any more and turned, got the door open. But as she did his hand was on her upper arm and it wasn't gentle as he grasped and swung her back to face him. The door slammed shut again, she had only a fraction of a second to see the blue ablaze and then he was so close and she shut her eyes. The kiss wasn't gentle either. It was hard and demanding and hurt.

But, as always, she softened for him, opened for him, couldn't say no to him. He could have her and take from her as much as he wanted. And then he softened too, his tongue caressing where moments before his mouth had pressed so fiercely, his fingers lightened on her arm and his lips soothed.

And at last she had the strength—she knew not from where—to twist away from him. He couldn't have everything from her when he wouldn't offer the same. It wasn't fair.

She turned, blindly groping for the door handle again, wrenching it open and scrambling into the seat.

'Drive.' It was sort of a bark but it ended as a broken sob. 'Please just drive.'

CHAPTER THIRTEEN

OWEN threw himself into work. He worked and worked and worked. And every minute of the day he thought about Bella. Missed her. Wondered what the hell she was doing—where she was, who she was with, whether she was happy, whether *she* was missing him. And then he worked some more.

He hadn't thought he had it in him to be so aware of another person. To be driven to meet their needs—to put someone before himself. He'd been so ignorant of his parents' situation, so wrapped up in himself and his ideals and ideas. Only now he saw how they and Liz had tainted his view of marriage and children.

He hadn't been in love with Liz. He'd never been in love with anyone until now. So of course back then he hadn't been ready for a child. The baby-that-wasn't hadn't ever seemed real to him, it had simply been the symbol of a burden he hadn't wanted then and thought he'd never want.

Now he knew that if Bella's child had been real he would have loved it—because now he knew what it was to love and how uncontrollable love could be.

When Liz had turned on him and told him how lonely he'd end up, he hadn't believed her. He'd never felt lonely. Too busy with his work. Too busy out partying when the need for physical company bit. He'd thought he had it all sussed.

Until now. Now he felt as lonely as it was possible to feel. And it hurt so badly he didn't know if he'd ever recover—he could only try to get used to it somehow.

He supposed it served him right. That the woman he'd found he was able to love wasn't one who needed it. The timing was all wrong. Her career was just starting. She was finally getting to where she'd wanted to be for so long. And he refused to ruin it for her. He didn't want her to resent him.

It was so ironic that when he finally found someone he wanted to care about, to love and cherish, help and protect, she was someone who was determined not to need those things. Bella didn't want help; she didn't want his money. She wanted independence. She'd said it, at the end there, that she needed to do this by herself. She was looking for respect. Trying to fight her family for it, fight him, every step of the way. But couldn't she see there was a balance? He couldn't stand back and watch her futile efforts when there were ways in which he could help. Maybe the way it had ended was all for the best.

Like hell it was.

As the days progressed, so his anger rose. Screw this true hero thing. It was a con. There was no happiness in nobility—not this sort. He should never have let her go, at least, not without him. She'd tipped his world upside down and then walked out, leaving him in a hell of a mess. Damn it, his wanting to help her wasn't because he thought she was incapable; it was about him simply wanting to support her. No one was truly independent—not even him.

And there he'd been worried he'd get bored with one person for life. He laughed, a bitter, self-mocking laugh. What an arrogant jerk. No one could ever be bored around Bella.

She was full of life—a little kooky perhaps, most definitely a touch accident-prone. But she was also true and sweet and generous and funny. He wanted the warmth she had to offer. And he didn't want to ever give it up.

He couldn't stop the emotion from flowering in him. She was his own magic fairy—she'd brought back his humanity, his humility, his hope. And he wanted to keep her by his side for ever. He chuckled. So he was still selfish. He was about to make his most selfish move ever.

The rehearsal weeks flew by. Bella had never worked so hard in all her life. They rehearsed all day and halfway through the evening. After that she collapsed into her little single bed in the tiny overcrowded flat that she was sharing with three other cast members and tried to sleep. Tried not to feel cold and lonely. But it was only when she closed her eyes tight and imagined herself in his big warm bed that she managed to drift off to sleep. In that blissful moment just on waking she'd still think she was there with him, but then she'd open her eyes and remember.

The work was full on but fun. She was glad she'd done all those years of dancing as a kid. Costumes were made, the set was designed, affairs were begun, gossip was spread. It was the mad, bad, bitchy world of musical theatre. She kept her distance from the worst of it. She learnt her part, understudied the other and developed an unhealthy obsession with the Internet. There was a lot on him—had she known she'd have looked sooner. But there was his website and a ton of articles about the savvy young entrepreneur. One of them had an accompanying picture of him in jeans and tee, totally looking like the relaxed guy she'd met that first night.

She couldn't indulge in her usual fix of chocolate, ice

cream and red wine without thinking of him, couldn't eat her muesli at odd times of the day, couldn't even have a coffee. Everywhere she turned, everything she did, she thought of him. But worst of all were the nights. When in her lonely, little bed she lay restless, remembering every moment, every move, every touch, every tease.

She worked harder, longer, not wanting her silly heart to ruin this time for her.

There was nothing, no contact from him, just as she'd requested. And she forced that stupid, still sparking hope inside to shrink—day by day.

Opening night was upon her before she knew it. Nerves threatened to swamp her. But as she put on her make-up the security guy came and delivered the most beautiful bunch of flowers to her. There was no note other than her name. No hint of who they might have come from. The speed of her pulse quadrupled. Were they from him? She got through the show on a buzz of adrenalin and bubbling hope. Was he out there—in the audience?

Afterwards she joined in the laughter and excitement of the others, then scurried back to her dressing room, changing into her opening-night party outfit. There was a knock at the door. Heart thundering, she opened it.

'Dad! Vita!' Her jaw dropped. 'It's you.'

'We wouldn't miss it for the world.' Vita threw her arms around her.

'I didn't think you even knew.' Bella emerged from the hug and looked from her father to her sister.

'Well, we wouldn't have if it was down to you.' Vita gave her a sharp look.

She hadn't thought they'd be that interested. Not that she was about to admit that to them.

'Did you get the flowers?' her father asked almost shyly.

'They were from you?' she asked in the wobbliest voice ever.

Her father nodded. 'Vita chose them.'

Her sister smiled at her.

Bella smiled back. She shouldn't feel disappointed. It was wonderful of them to have sent them. It was even more wonderful that they'd been here for her. But she'd wanted to believe they'd been from Owen. Crushed, she forced out a smile. Her best acting job of the night was required *after* the performance.

'We're coming again when you get to Auckland,' her father said unexpectedly.

Vita nodded enthusiastically. 'To a matinee when you're playing the lead. All the brothers are coming too. We've booked out a whole block of seats.'

Bella failed on the smile front then, bent her head to hide the sudden tears that were stinging her eyes. She blinked a few times. 'How did you know about that?'

'Someone sent us the details.' Her father spoke.

'Oh?'

'Owen sent an email to the whole family,' Vita said.

'What?' But there was no time for a repeat—now that her father had started talking, it seemed he couldn't stop.

'You were great up there, honey. I was so proud.' He beamed. 'Your mother would have loved it.'

She couldn't hide the tears then, and her father awkwardly put his arm around her, offering her a comfort she hadn't had in years.

Vita and Bella sat while their dad went up to the counter to get drinks at the after show party.

'You know, I've always been a bit jealous of you.' Vita smiled. 'Now I'm a lot.'

Nonplussed, Bella just stared at her for a moment. 'You want to be onstage?'

Vita laughed. 'No!' She shook her head. 'All that make-up would play havoc with my skin,' she joked. 'No, it was because you always seemed so confident. You didn't give a damn about what the rest of us were doing, or what Dad thought you should do. You just knew what you wanted and went for it. You've got such determination.'

'You've got to be kidding me.' Bella nearly choked. 'It's not like that at all.'

'But you've always known what you wanted,' Vita said. 'I've never known. I only did commerce because it was what everyone else had done and they seemed to do OK.'

Yes, but the fantasy of what Bella had wanted and the reality weren't panning out to be quite the same thing. 'Is it OK?' she asked her sister.

'Yeah, but I'm not exactly passionate about it.' Vita winked. 'Spreadsheets and tax returns aren't exactly something you live for.' She laughed. 'Whereas you have a job you love. I'm envious of that. But—' she leant forward '—I've got a secret. I'm quitting accountancy and I'm opening my own café.'

'You're what?' Bella was astounded. 'Vita, do you know how hard it is to work in a café?'

'Sure.'

'What does Hamish say?'

Vita's eyes glowed. 'He's really supportive. It's because of him that I'm finally going to do it. I'm doing a catering course and then I'm opening up. He's keeping an eye out for a good location now. He's such a great guy, Bella.'

'I know.' Bella nodded. 'Wow. That's really cool. Good for you.'

'I'd never have had the guts if I didn't have you as an example, though.'

Bella nearly laughed. If only her sister knew. It had only been because of Owen that she'd got the part. He'd made her so mad. Worst of all he'd been right. But she couldn't think of him any more. 'Thanks so much for coming to the show. And for bringing Dad. I really appreciate it.'

'It was Owen who organised it. What's happening with him anyway?'

'Oh, nothing,' Bella answered shortly, really not wanting to dwell on him. 'We're just friends.'

Vita giggled. 'As if. The two of you the night before my wedding? My God, you had the place steaming up so bad there was practically water running down the walls.'

Bella felt her cheeks blaze.

'He's very good-looking,' Vita said. 'And very successful.'

'What do you know about him?' She couldn't stop her curiosity.

'Bella—' Vita shook her head '—if you were remotely clued in to the real world like the rest of us you'd know too. He made squillions when he sold his web stuff to that multimedia conglomerate.' She looked sly. 'How did the two of you meet anyway?'

Bella shook her head. She sure didn't want to go there. 'It was nothing. It's over. This was just him being nice.'

'I don't think a guy like Owen would be organising your family for you if it was over—he wouldn't want us getting the wrong idea.'

'I haven't spoken to him in weeks. Trust me, it's over.' This last gesture was just the way he worked, charming to the end, still helping her out. Only now she was trying even harder to forget the heat in that final kiss, trying to stop wondering what might have happened if she hadn't got the part, if she hadn't left town.

Thankfully her father was heading to the table carrying a tray laden with glasses and nibbles. Talk returned to the show and the tour.

She got to the theatre early as usual the next day.

'This parcel arrived for you last night too—sorry I didn't get it to you sooner.' The security guy at the theatre door collared her as she made her way in.

'Oh, that's fine,' she answered, heart hammering as she recognised the handwriting on the packet, trying not to snatch the thing out of his hands. She hurried to her dressing room, ripped the end of the bag and tipped the contents out.

A soft toy tiger bounced onto the table. She picked up the plush creature. There was a small card on a ribbon around his neck. She read it. 'Break a leg.'

She didn't need her leg breaking as well, thanks very much. She already had a broken heart. That was more than enough. She tipped the bag upside down and shook it again. Nothing else. No other message. It wasn't even signed. There was no return address on the back.

Bastard. She tossed the tiger across the room. She'd asked him not to contact her, all the while been hoping he would and now he had and with what—a damn toy? For the child he thought she was? She'd wanted more—she'd wanted so much more. This almost felt worse than nothing.

Almost. She frowned at the tiger. Why had she thought that he'd taken her seriously? But for about five minutes there he'd really seemed to want to believe in her and her party business. Hell, he'd even offered to help her paint a jungle mural on his warehouse wall, for heaven's sake.

So what did he mean by this? She was too scared to try to figure it out and too stupid not to start hoping some more.

The tiger seemed to be looking at her reproachfully. She rolled her eyes. It was a toy, for goodness' sake. Inanimate. *Stuffed.* The reproachful look deepened.

'Oh, all right, then.' She stomped over to it. 'Stop making me feel so guilty.' She picked him up, fingers automatically smoothing his fur. 'Don't think you're sleeping in my bed, though.'

The nights started to blur together. After the excitement of the opening, the thrill of the first reviews, they settled into the performances, tried not to get stale. And the reality of her new life hit her.

She was lonely. The show lasted nearly two hours. The applause lasted maybe ten minutes at the most. There was no real contact or interaction with the audience. The cast and crew were fabulous, fun. They were a kind of family. But she couldn't quite get into it. Why was it that things were never quite how you imagined they would be?

Early in the mornings that followed, she snuggled deeper into her bed, hugged Tiger that little bit closer, and dreamed.

CHAPTER FOURTEEN

IT WAS the matinee performance and Bella was taking the lead for the first time. She swallowed her nerves, but found they got stuck in her throat. So she stood in the wings and remembered the fierce look on Owen's face when he'd told her she had to believe in herself.

Believe. Believe. Believe.

As the opening music started she closed her eyes, whispered it to herself one more time and then stepped onto the stage. Looking on it afterwards, the whole thing was a blur. But backstage everyone was effusive in their congratulations and support. Even the director was pleased and told her that if she kept up like that she'd be getting bigger parts very soon. Bittersweet success flavoured her mood as she tripped down the corridor to the dressing rooms.

She stopped. Owen was leaning against the wall outside her door.

She stared. Looked him up and down and up and down and again. Put a hand out to balance herself against the wall because her legs had gone lifeless.

At her dumbfounded appraisal his grin was boyish. 'My mother taught me to dress for the theatre.'

'Even the eleven a.m. matinee show with all the audience aged either under ten or over sixty?'

'It's still the theatre,' he said smoothly.

She took a step closer. The tuxedo was devastating. The jacket fitting so well across his broad shoulders and tapering into his lean hips it just had to have been tailor-made.

Finally her heart started beating again—loud, painful thumping. 'What are you doing here?' She couldn't believe it.

'You were great.' He'd lost the grin and was now serious and not quite meeting her eyes.

'What are you doing here?' She strained to focus. She had to know.

'You really were amazing on that stage.'

He spoke so softly, she almost wondered if he was talking to her or just himself.

'Are you listening to me?' What the hell was going on?

'You have a real gift.'

She couldn't handle any more of this madness.

'I'm getting changed.' She stalked straight past him, into the dressing room, and shut the door. She whipped off her costume, climbed into her usual skirt and top, and wiped off as much of the make-up as she could in thirty seconds. Then she stared at her reflection in the mirror. Had she just imagined that encounter? Was she finally going nuts?

Taking a deep, supposedly stabilising breath, she opened the door. He was leaning against the jamb right in front of her. The tux was no less magnificent. Her brain went fuzzy.

He straightened. 'Can we go somewhere to talk?'

She searched his features, wanting him to meet her gaze. 'Why are you here?'

He looked at her then, blue eyes blazing. 'Why do you think?'

She expelled a sharp breath as everything inside quivered.

She fought the sensation, tensing up—that *look* wasn't enough. She wanted to hear it. Wanted to *know*—because what he was here for might not be enough for her. Anger and uncertainty and fear ripped through the delight in seeing him. 'Are you ready to define us yet, Owen? Or are we still not applying labels?'

He glanced away, down the corridor, and she realised he too was tense all over. 'Just give me a minute, Bella.'

'You're kidding,' she snapped. 'How much time do you need?'

'Listen to you.' His sharp smile flashed. 'You really have got your act together.'

'Don't you patronise me.' Frustration trammelled through her. She was ready to slam the door again—in his face.

But in a swift movement he put his hands on her hips and jerked her out of the doorway towards him. 'Never.'

One arm snaked hard around her waist, pulling her home, while his other hand lifted, holding her head up to his as his mouth descended. Her body thudded into his as their lips connected and just like that her fight against him was gone, overtaken completely by desire and ultimately by love.

She was holding her head up all by herself and his hands were all over her, pressing, pulling her closer to his heat and strength. And still it wasn't close enough. Shaking, she threaded her fingers through his hair, holding him, clutching at him, reaching up on tiptoe as her mouth clung to his—giving, seeking, taking, wanting more and more. Pure energy, electricity, sent sparks through her where they touched. She moaned into his mouth, feeling his response—harder, fiercer, deeper. The madness was back and she wanted it to last for ever.

He was the one who eased them out of it. His large hands taking her wrists, lowering them as he slowly lifted his head.

For a second she strained up to follow. And then she heard it—the cacophony, the riot. She glanced to the side.

Oh, God, the entire cast and crew were in the corridor, watching them, catcalling and wolf-whistling and cheering.

She turned back and tried to tug free from his grip. She knew her cheeks were scarlet.

'I did ask you to give me a minute.' He grinned at her, but his hands were still tight, keeping her close. 'To get us some privacy. But now I'm not letting go.'

'My flat,' she muttered. 'It's only a few minutes away.'

He guided her out of the theatre, holding her hand firmly. Still flushed, she could hardly summon a smile for her colleagues as they called goodbye, wished her well and made the odd laughingly crude comment.

'And there was me thinking you liked an audience,' Owen said dryly as they got outside. He opened the door to the waiting taxi. She didn't question, just got in and gave the driver the address. Owen slid in the back seat beside her, reclaimed her hand and passed the time chatting to the taxi driver about the rugby.

But he said nothing as, trembling, she unlocked the door and led the way in. And when she turned in the tiny room and saw him behind her, looking at her with those brilliant eyes, the loneliness and heartache that she'd tried so hard to bury resurfaced in a crashing wave, crushing her. She couldn't believe that he was here. And what if he still couldn't give her everything she wanted? She couldn't settle for less, but she had no choice. She was so bound to him, had such need for him, it terrified her. She blinked as her eyes stung, but still the world went blurry.

'Ah, Bella.' Husky, he reached for her, took her into his arms, wrapping them around her—strong and secure. 'I'm sorry.'

She burrowed her face into his broad chest, gripped his lapels, a bundle of tension and fearful need.

But he said nothing more. For long moments he just cradled her gently, stroking his hand down her rigid back in a long, slow rhythm, until at last she felt her warmth returning, and could relax into him. His arms tightened.

And then she was the one who spoke. 'Vita and my dad came to the show.'

'I know.'

'Opening night.'

'I know.'

'They're coming again, when I'm the lead in Auckland.'

'I know.'

More tears leaked from her eyes. It had all been him. 'It means a lot to me.'

'I know.'

She took in a deep breath, shuddered with it. 'Thank you.' It was muffled, into his shoulder.

His fingers slid up, into her hair. His mouth moved on the top of her head. 'They loved it. They love you.'

'I know.'

'He just wants you to be happy.'

'Yeah.'

'He thought that what made them happy would be the same thing to make you happy. But you're different, Bella. You're you. And you had to work it out for yourself.'

She nodded. 'But what I thought would make me happy hasn't.'

He lifted her chin, frowning at her tear-stained face. 'You're not happy?'

She shook her head. 'Owen, I'm such a mess.' Another tear spilt. 'I thought I wanted all this, but I don't.'

He looked deep into her eyes. 'What do you want?'

You. She was sure he could read her answer. But she refused to say it; it sounded so pathetic. And he wasn't all she wanted. She still wanted everything. 'I'm not going to do the Australian leg of the tour. I'll do New Zealand, but that's it. It's not what I want to do.'

His frown returned, bigger than before. 'But, Bella—'

'I miss the kids,' she interrupted, wanting to explain before she lost the nerve. 'I miss the direct contact. It's make-up on, bright lights, but I can hardly see the audience. It's a big theatre but it seems lonely. They applaud, they leave. By the time I'm scrubbed and changed, there's no one there. There's no interaction.' She lifted her chin, determined to take pride in her decision. 'I know being a children's entertainer isn't exactly the most highly rated job there is, but I'm good with them. I enjoy it. I'm going to go ahead and find my own venue and set up a business like you suggested. It was a good idea.'

He smiled then, a warm, encouraging smile. 'Bella, that's wonderful.'

Pleasure washed through her as she heard and saw his support. He believed in her and how she loved him for it and suddenly nothing else mattered. She'd take whatever he had, for however long, it would be enough—because she loved him.

'Don't look at me like that,' he suddenly begged. 'I'm not kissing you again until I've said what I have to say.'

She leaned that little closer into him and he groaned.

'I'm coming on tour with you.' He blurted the words out.

'What?' She jerked upright again.

'I'm coming with you. Sorry if that's not what you want, but that's what's happening.' He spoke even faster. 'I'm not spending another night apart from you.' He bent his head. 'Ever.'

She gasped at the rush of exhilaration. This kiss was even

hungrier and more desperate than the one at the theatre. They clung, fierce, fevered. But again slowly, reluctantly, he drew back. He gripped her hands, stopping their frantic exploration, making her listen.

'I can work with my laptop and mobile. I'll have to fly to meetings every now and then, but I'll be back for the night. Every night.'

She couldn't stop the smile spreading as the glow inside grew stronger, becoming a solid flame of joy. 'OK.'

'And another thing,' he continued after another crazy kiss, his hands failing to stop their own exploration this time, 'the next family wedding you're going to is your own.'

'I thought you didn't believe in marriage.' She gaped. 'That it wasn't worth the paper it was written on.'

'You remember every stupid thing I've ever said, don't you?' he asked ruefully.

'Some of it wasn't so stupid.' He'd changed her life, made her see everything so much clearer. And now her whole body seemed to be singing.

'I want to marry you,' he said softly. 'I'll never want anyone but you. But I need you to tell me if you're not happy and I've not noticed.'

'You'll notice,' she assured him. 'You notice more about me than I do myself.'

'But if I'm buried in work...' He stopped, then almost whispered, 'I don't want to fail you.'

'You won't.' She raised her hand to his cheek, gently smiling. 'And if you do, I can always send you an email.'

'You'd do that?' He chuckled. 'For me?'

'I'd do anything for you,' she quietly admitted, knowing he already knew that.

His arms tightened. 'I never thought I could love anyone

the way I love you.' At last she saw the vulnerability in his eyes as he wholly opened up. 'I want to be everything for you.'

'You already are.'

He shook his head. 'I want to do everything with you. I want to give you everything.' He drew in a shaky breath. 'I want you to have our children, Bella. I want your children.'

At that she closed her burning eyes tight, pressed them hard against his jacket again. 'Me too,' she said, and then drew a deep breath. 'But maybe not for a while? I want to make the business work first.' And she wanted to have some time just with him, to broaden their foundations before they had their family.

'OK. You just say the word. When you're ready, I'll be ready.'

He was going to be there for her, for everything.

She reached up, pulled him down for her kiss and walked backwards, leading him to her tiny bedroom. He glanced around and she melted at the mix of relief and desire in his face. Her legs stumbled and he scooped her up.

'Do me a favour.' He lifted his mouth from hers for a moment.

'Anything.' She pulled it back to her.

'When we get home, can you put on that bridesmaid's dress?'

She paused then. 'It's hideous.'

He shook his head. 'It's beautiful.'

She undid his tie. 'Your eyesight is dodgy from all that staring at screens.'

'You have no idea the number of fantasies I've had involving that dress. All these long, lonely nights where I've had nothing but those pictures.' He stole another quick kiss. 'You have no idea how much I regret missing that wedding. I totally fell for you the minute I saw you in that bar—it was like nothing else. I should have held onto you then and there. Never let you go.'

She melted more. 'It happened right. You were right. I needed to stand up and try. To discover what it was I wanted.'

'And so did I.' He turned and leaned back, landing them both on her bed. But he didn't kiss her; instead he reached behind him, sliding his hand under the sheet and pulling out... Tiger.

Owen's whole expression softened, the lights in his eyes warming, mouth twitching. 'So you got him.'

She nodded. 'He usually comes to the theatre with me but the others were joking about him and I was worried he'd go wandering.'

'Well, sorry, tiger, there's no room in here any more.' He bent his arm back, about to throw him.

'Don't you dare!' Bella scolded, taking the toy from him. 'He's been a good friend to me these past few days.'

'Have you been cuddling him?'

'Maybe.' She tried to play it cool.

He grinned and took the toy from her. 'What a good little tiger, keeping her arms occupied and scaring off any interlopers.'

'As if I'd do that.'

'It wasn't you I was worried about,' he teased. 'It was all these showbiz boys and crew and groupies. They'll all be panting after you.'

'Half of them are gay.'

'And half of them aren't. I wanted tiger here to be the only thing in your arms. And you did a good job, didn't you, boy? Well, I'm back now and you can go sleep somewhere else.'

He stood up and put the tiger on an armchair, facing away from the bed, slung her cardigan over him.

'Happy now?' His eyes were twinkling.

'No,' she answered—all tragedy—but she couldn't hide the happiness any more. It burst out of her. 'Not until you're back here.'

He vaulted onto the bed, kissed her and their passion, too long denied, erupted. As he rose, his strong body braced over hers, she spread her fingers wide across his chest and marvelled. She simply couldn't believe she was going to have it all.

'How did I get so lucky?'

'It isn't luck, Bella,' he muttered as he pushed home. 'It's what you deserve.' He drew closer still. 'You deserve everything.'

She arched, reaching to meet him, wanting to give him as much as he was giving her, so that together they would have it all. And, as his murmurs of love melded to her moans, and the feeling of bliss between their bodies grew, she knew.

She'd succeeded.

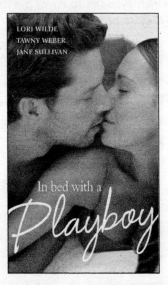

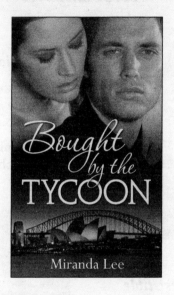

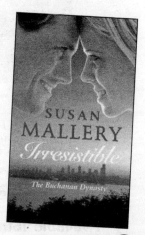

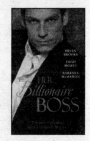